REAPER

Copyright 2017 Thea Atkinson
Published by Thea Atkinson
Edited by Laura Kingsley

Cover art by gwendolyn1.deviantart.com
Typography by Thea Atkinson

A SPECIAL THANKS

I want to thank Terri Roller who beta read an early draft for me. She was instrumental in helping with the CPR details as well as picking out quite a few extra spaces and voice recognition errors. Pretty much saved my bacon. A special thanks goes to Robie, who cleaned up the rest of the picky things.

Thanks!

THANKS FOR CHECKING ME OUT

CHAPTER 1

The text was simple: it said to come to the church and to come alone.

I took one look at the purple text balloons and knew who they were from right away, even though I hadn't heard from Sarah for well over two years.

I chewed my lip, trying to decide what would make Sarah text me after all this time. She'd been one of the girls I'd fostered with in a halfway house before my grandfather petitioned successfully for my custody. That was what? Three years ago? She'd been a damaged girl even then. Deeply damaged. In the long hours of dark nights, she'd told me tales of the home she'd been 'rescued' from. Bad enough stories that I'd always wondered if that's all they were until the courts decreed she could go home and she'd elected to run away instead.

By the time I left with my grandfather to live with him three states away, they still hadn't found her. I'd always felt guilty about leaving her behind and in those first weeks I texted her dozens of times. Each time I sent off a text and spent long days waiting for a reply, I was haunted by the memory of those stories of hers. Witchcraft rituals that involved all sorts of blood rites and animal cruelty were the lightest of them. Sometimes she even hinted at sexual deviance and torture. Each memory sent my fingers to the keypad again with another quick text. She never responded.

Until this morning.

That she was texting me after going dark all those months ago could only mean one thing. She was in trouble. Trouble was something I understood well. Anyone who ended up in foster care did. And if she needed me, I wouldn't let a little thing like a crazy scary church keep me away, even if it was midnight.

I twisted my ankle back and forth in my combat boots as I worked up my courage to go in. Standing in front of the thing, it wasn't quite so easy to stomp up the broad stone steps and push my way through the doors. It was downright creepy. There was only a single lamp light to illuminate it and if in my mind I thought I could call it little, my eyesight certainly couldn't. It was gargantuan. Even in the street light the gargoyles squatting over its façade seemed to be leering at me. I pulled in a bracing breath then let it go with a hiss because there really were no other options. I was going in. I owed Sarah. She'd shown me the ropes of foster care, even showed me a thing or two about fighting. Because of her, I had fast hands and a snappy punch. I had skills. I could handle myself. Sort of. And after all of that, she had ended up with the dirty side of the lunch tray while I got to go to a home that pretty much served a banquet up to me on a silver platter each and every day.

I couldn't just leave her in there, shivering and cold and hungry. I'd brought the peanut butter and banana sandwich, hadn't I? It sat in my overcoat pocket, emitting its fruity smell every time I took a step. Surely, I'd made the decision already.

I shook my hands out. I could do this. I should. There was nothing truly frightening about the church. I'd been in it plenty of times during the day. It was old, yes. Very old. No one cared about the beauty it might have been in its day. Instead, someone had come in long before I'd arrived and set fire to whatever they could find that would burn. I knew if I touched the wood of the pews, they would be scorched and blistered. It's just that nighttime was different. Things seemed more frightening in the dark. Everything held a hidden threat.

Going inside meant simply stomping with purpose up the broad stone steps and walking through the ornately carved wooden door that hung on its hinges like a drunken man against its cracked and splintered partner. The streetlamp on the sidewalk bathed the Gothic church with enough light that I could see the wrought iron hoop door handles were bleeding old rust onto the wood. Didn't matter. I wouldn't need to yank the doors open or push them apart. The gap was big enough between the two I could squeeze right through. I didn't bother to try pulling them tight together again behind me. Instead, I paused just on the other side, letting my eyes adjust to the gloom.

The church smelled of old wood and moldy vestments. I imagined some cloistered monk in days gone by pulling on a robe over his homespun cassock, transforming himself into something more worthy of prayer than the thing he looked like on a regular day to his parishioners. The town of Dyre in those days no doubt had its share of fearful citizens who became ever more fearful at the sight of the cloth-of-gold trim that transformed their lowly priest into a demigod. Even one of the broken stained glass windows showed some hapless priest during the rite of communion glowing as the host touched his tongue.

My boots shot off noises like a trapped bat's echolocation, bouncing off the altar and throwing themselves back at me with an almost haunting tone. I stomped my foot once to show the church I wasn't afraid.

I tried out my voice.

"Sarah?"

Nothing. At least I didn't sound afraid. That was something.

I panned my cell phone flashlight over the ceiling where the glow from the streetlights couldn't reach. Mostly made of stone and wrought iron fixtures, the church had been abandoned in the early part of the century. Word was it was too hard to heat. Too expensive to keep up. No one used it anymore but the town loved having the creepy old thing as a landmark. It was even on their postcards. Yet, no one took care of the place. Hadn't in years, it seemed. Its dozen chandeliers either had fallen to the floor beneath the glower of squatting gargoyles, unable to grip the ceiling when their chains rusted through, or they still clung to their hooks with tenacious fingers of iron. I resolved to steer clear of those. None looked very safely pinned to their places anymore. In fact, the whole damn place looked like a death trap.

I hugged my chest, shivering a bit as I called out again.

"Sarah, are you there?"

Still nothing.

I peered sideways at the stained glass windows, where a streetlight pierced the gloom. Long broken, most of them, and shattered into pieces on the tiled floor. I took a step sideways and heard glass crunch beneath my boot. I lifted my toe and shone my cell down at it. A section of window had fallen unbroken to the tiles only to end up a casualty beneath my right foot. Pity. It had been beautiful once. An angel, I thought, careening to earth with fire on its wings. I lifted my gaze to the altar ahead of me.

"Sarah, it's Ayla."

I had just decided to inspect the gallery above when I caught scent of something unusual. Smoke. Not old smoke left over from the ages old arson, either, but fragrant, curling, new smoke.

The hairs on the back of my neck prickled to attention. I thought I felt a small pressure at the small of my back that trailed upward like a lazy finger to the spot right where my ribcage connected to my spine. Everything in my body went clammy. I didn't dare swallow for fear of making a noise. It was irrational to be afraid when I knew no one stood behind me, but I was.

"Stop fooling around," I said, twisting to see behind me, and when nothing met my gaze, I aimed my cell phone off to my right.

The confessionals loomed out from the darkness. No doubt Sarah was kneeling on one of those wooden benches and peering through the grills at me. Trying to scare me.

"That incense has to be a hundred years old," I said, claiming what was left of my bravado and stomping up the aisle toward the booth. "Who knows what germs you're letting go by burning it."

I paused at the face of the threadbare curtain. She was in there, alright. I could just make out the gleam of her irises in my cell phone light. I tried on a matronly tone to encourage her out of there and into the aisle.

"You're gonna get sick."

Small puffs wafted out at me. Sickly sweet. I coughed without meaning to.

"Seriously," I said, waving the stink from my face. "Plague, Black death."

"They're the same thing," said a voice.

A long pause drew itself out as my mind tried to work

through the fact that the voice coming from behind the curtain was not the one I expected. Heck. It wasn't even feminine. I had the feeling I was suspended in time. Some alternate universe had slipped up through the cracks in the floor and wrapped itself around my ankles, holding me there. There was a moment when I almost felt as though I was falling backwards through empty sky, waiting for the moment when I would strike the earth, and in that second I felt a strange elation. Then terror.

I jammed my hand into my pocket, feeling for the sandwich to assure myself that I was indeed awake. Yes. It was there. It squished beneath my grip and oozed through the cellophane into my fingers.

It wasn't until a deep and dark chuckle came from behind the curtain that my brain finally hiccoughed into life. That laughter sounded as though it was made of the same cloying smoke that streamed out through the gap in the curtain. I got the impression I was smelling burnt sugar.

I think my breath froze in a solid clump. I know my feet had. I certainly couldn't swallow down past the hard lump it made in my throat. Thankfully, my reflexes worked and the heel of my hand snapped forward. Every part of my psyche sagged in relief when I felt it connect with what I hoped was a nose. Broken or not, I couldn't waste any time. That was how the actresses in movies ended up dead. They waited around to investigate. Not this chick. This chick was out of there.

Didn't matter who was inside the confessional. Didn't

matter if he had Sarah tied up in there with him. Self preservation came first. Whether or not I wanted to stay to help Sarah, my legs had other ideas.

I fell twice as I stampeded for the door, stumbling over the shards of glass and ramming into the edges of the pews as I vaulted forward. For same reason, my feet slid all over the place and I ended up running in place for three full heartbeats before I caught some tread and tore for the narthex. Even then I slid all over the place as though my boots had run into a slick of oil.

A slick of oil. Even registering the words made me realize that's exactly what I had stepped in--no doubt just outside the confessional--and it was making my retreat clumsy and ineffectual. I gave a brief thought to Sarah, wondering if she had encountered the same mess. If she had fallen. If she was in here somewhere with a broken ankle or something. I yelled her name again, praying I would hear her respond.

Whatever was behind me chuckled again and then I did scream. I let go a holler that hurt my ears and I threw myself at each pew, gripping the backs for propulsion because my feet failed to navigate the slippery floor. I was all over the place and I was nowhere all at once.

I whimpered when I realized I wasn't making much progress and nearly fell. Whoever was behind me shouted some word that at once sounded both foreign and vaguely familiar. It was as though he thought I would understand it.

"Who the heck are you?" I yelled over my shoulder at

him. "What do you want?"

"You," he said.

Me. A whimper rose from my throat at the word. If that comment was meant to terrify me, it did. I was a soaking mess of fear. A thousand horrible thoughts jumped onto the tracks of my mind and rode them with wild abandon. It was just a matter of time before they came to a crashing halt and flew out into the rhubarb.

"What have you done with Sarah?" I said, thinking I might at least be able to buy myself some time as I tried to find solid footing. So what if my voice was breaking on every word? At least I wasn't screaming uncontrollably. Not yet.

I slid again and caught myself just before I fell. I swore at myself. I had to stop panicking. It wasn't getting me anywhere. I could do this. I could. I had to.

I scrambled for solid footing, digging with the tips of my combat boots into the floor and slipping again. I laughed out loud like a fool when I went down again. I bit down on my tongue. I tasted blood. I thought I heard the rattling sound of hoarse breathing. That breath was reaching out for me, I just knew it. It was a real live thing with hands and intent and touch. I knew it would grip the back of my neck if I didn't do something.

I spun around, straining with wide eyes into the shadows to catch sight of him. I needed to see how close he was. If he was coming at me, let him come at me while I could see him.

"Stay back," I said, and even as I raised my hands to

ward him off, I was frantically eyeballing the shadows.

There had to be something in here that I could grab. Throw at him. Swing at him. Nothing anywhere near. I kicked at the glass around me, lifting shards to the air, but they just tinkled to the floor a few feet short of striking him. In desperation, I dug into my pocket and pulled out the sandwich and hurled it in his general direction. It sailed past him and made a splat somewhere on the tiles behind him.

Foolish. Even if it had struck him, what would that have done? I needed something better. I groped around in the darkness in a frenzy to lay my hands on something. Anything.

I froze. I had my cell phone.

I could dial the police.

My hands fumbled to turn on the screen and swipe in the keypad.

By then the maniac had stepped into the light streaming through one of the broken windows. I thought I caught sight of a face filled with tattoos. He was bald, I knew that. It took me several seconds to realize that the markings on his face covered every inch of his skin and it was only as I realized this that I understood he was naked from the waist up. I had the ridiculous thought that the tattoos went all the way to his toes.

That wasn't normal. At least not any side of normal I'd ever seen.

Something deep in my chest squeezed as though it was a wet rag being wrung clean of water. Pay attention, I told myself. Get help.

I tapped numbers on the screen, thinking they were a nine, a one and a one. Nothing happened. I'd typed in an eight, a seven and a two.

I sobbed. This couldn't be happening. I could dial any number I wanted to at any time without even looking at the screen. What was wrong with me now that I couldn't do that small thing?

When the screen went dark my legs finally gave way and I staggered onto my knees. A shard of glass dug its way into my kneecap.

"Sweet Jesus," I heard myself murmur and tried to stand again.

"Not the chosen one, no," he said. "Oh, no. Nowhere near Jesus."

He flicked his wrist toward me and in a second of instinct, I ducked. Something wet and greasy splashed into my hair and ran down my neck.

I clawed my way to a stand with the liquid running down beneath my shirt and soaking my chest. There was no way I was going to die there. Not at the hands of some psychopath when I had been on a mission of mercy. Not when my grandfather had no idea where I was. I would live. I would get the hell out of there. Bleeding or not, I'd make my legs move.

I tried. I gave it every bit of muscle I could.

They wouldn't obey. And that was when I knew he had done something to me with that oil. I had no idea what or even how, but a timid squirrel in the jungles of my memory peeked out long enough to tell me I'd been a fool not to have reacted to that liquid assault.

I was stuck somewhere between the galley and the narthex. I could see the door. It yawned open enough that the streetlights cut through the shadows and illuminated the floor in front of me. I noticed my boot was on the pretty face of the angel again. The flames licked around its wings in the glass scene. I saw my reflection in the darker places of glass. I looked terrified. Flaming red hair spilled over the reflection of the angel as it went careening downward and for a second looked just like the flames licking at its wings.

The image initiated a sucking sound in the back of my mind, like a sink unclogging. Terror. That was it. I'd never felt such fear. It made my breath come in harsh rasps.

I scented something heavily fragrant. Myrrh, my mind told me, and yet I had no idea how I might know the smell.

I twisted away, working through the air as though it was chest deep water. What if I drowned in my own adrenaline, lost all ability to move? I'd be stuck here. At his mercy. I gagged on a drag of air in desperation. I'd swim to the exit if I had to.

"*Corum Deo*," he said from behind me. "*Infinitum mortis.*"

"Shut up," I screamed and whipped around to hurl my phone at him. It struck him on the cheek and bounced off, clattering to the tiles and coming to a rest three feet from me. Three feet from him too. Oh my god, he was just a quick sprint away. I tried to scream but only managed a small squeak of fear.

"It's futile to run," he said and I thought I heard a note of relief in his voice. "You're mine. My last fare. I get to go home now. Finally."

He was talking in riddles. A psychopath if ever there was one. Yet something in his voice caught my attention. The words, the concept was familiar. Home. Last fare. I met his eye and for one long moment we stared at each other, and then I followed his gaze upward, to the heavens.

It was then that I noticed the ash falling from the sky. Large, gossamer flakes of it drifted down from an unseen source. Was the sky burning and dropping bits of singed cloud to the earth? It certainly looked like it was burning.

"Feathers," he said. "From a blessed raven." He cocked his head at me as though I should understand what that meant.

A feather landed on my shoulder. I reached for it, dumbfounded, and discovered it was wet. Scented.

"Cypress oil," he said. "And sandalwood."

"Oil?" I said, confused. Past the terror, the bewilderment had its own sort of paralysis.

He nodded slowly. "And holy fire," he said. "You remember." He looked up.

I followed his gaze as though it was a magnet and realized why I thought the sky was burning.

The cathedral was on fire.

CHAPTER 2

I should have run. I knew I should. But all I could do was gawk at the flames as they crackled above me, chewing through the old wood of the gallery's banister and casting an eerie light onto the stucco ceiling above it. I wondered if someone else was up there setting everything to light while the psychopath was trying to ensnare me down here. I wondered why I was a target in the first place. Maybe it was Sarah up there. Maybe she had decided that I'd had it too good all these years while she'd been on the run and wanted me to suffer for it.

It certainly didn't sound like Sarah, but I couldn't work out the significance of why I was here and connect it with her except to think that she must've been involved somehow. I was still trying to work through the confusion when a flaming chunk of wooden railing fell with a horrific thud just a foot in front of me. The flames caught the edge of an oil slick and blazed higher. Three others sparked to life as well. One to my left, to my right, and if I craned to peer over my shoulder, two to my back. Like corners. Just seeing them blazing all around me was enough to free my muscles from their paralysis. They seemed to understand even if my brain didn't that I would be trapped here if I didn't move. Burned alive. A fissure in the paralysis opened up, one large enough for me to crawl through.

I put my feet to work shuffling back in an effort to reach the door without taking my eye off that quietly advancing form. I butted up against something hard. The door. Thank all the gods great and small. I hadn't realized I was close to the exit but I wasn't about to question it. I was literally feet from freedom. I stole a look over my shoulder to see him still standing there, arms crossed as though he was on a leisurely stroll.

I spun around, fully intending to flee straight out the door, and leave the maniac to brave the fire on his own. I planned to pound my combat boots on the asphalt all the way to Old Yeller, and get the heck out of there. Cell phone be damned. I'd get it in the morning. With a dozen police men at my heels.

That was when I realized I was nowhere near the door at all. I stared through open-air all the way through the several remaining feet to that drunken looking door and its pitiful partner. Whatever was keeping me from progressing, it wasn't because anything was in the way. It was impossible, and yet, I couldn't break through.

"No," I said, telling myself I was just in shock. One thrust and I could launch myself at the door. Whatever I had felt, whatever barrier I believed I'd butted up against was nothing but terror. There was the door. There was the open air in front of it. I just needed to get to it. I took a running step. Nothing. I thrust myself forward as though I was running at a door. Again, I was propelled backward.

It was ridiculous that I couldn't break through the open space.

I launched myself toward the space between myself and the door and slammed against something hard again. I shouldered it. Kicked it.

I hugged myself, glancing frantically around me at the fire's blazing in every corner. The heat from it was already making me break out into a sweat.

It was no use. However impossible it might be, the air was as solid as the stone walls around me.

"It's foolish to run," he said, following me. "You can't get past the spelled oil."

"Spelled oil," I said, drawing out the words as though they could somehow explain to me what was going on, but only registering his statement that I couldn't run. That it was useless. My skin went cold despite the heat of the fires around me. If I couldn't run, I'd end up burning to death. Burning. To. Death.

I swallowed but the liquid flooding my cheeks wouldn't stay down. I thought shadows had started to creep into the edges of my vision. I was aware that I'd begun to gasp at the air.

I ran my hands over the air in front of me, feeling ridiculously like an untalented mime. What met my palms was solid and invisible.

"Can't be," I said.

A sob escaped me. This couldn't be happening. None of this could be happening.

The flames were rising on my left. I could feel the heat of the burning oil heating my cheeks and making my hair stick from sweat to my temples. The crackling of the wood in the gallery above me as it was consumed by the flames sang in my ears. Even the slightest sounds were magnified: the footsteps of that psychopath behind me, creeping up on me as though he wanted to torture me by making me wait for him to reach me.

"Don't worry," he said. "No doubt you'll just come back as a human again. Maybe not with that demonic red hair, but--"

I didn't wait to hear the rest. I started to scream. Long and loud and exhausting ever bit of air in my lungs. My entire body spasmed with the effort. I had to get someone to hear me.

The fire grew. It lit up the cathedral with its wavering light, and I could see my attacker as clearly as if he was strolling through a perfectly well lit church on a bright summer's day.

He was indeed covered in tattoos. I wasn't sure if I should feel relief at knowing my vision wasn't betraying me or if it should worry me more. All I knew was the way my stomach squeezed at noticing those marks had been inked onto his eyelids, showing themselves clearly when he blinked. They were even on the palms of his hand when he stretched toward me. Swirling symbols inched their way down his chest and disappeared beneath the waistband of his pants. Each one of them was deep and dark. Too dark to be regular ink. I was reminded of my foster care creativity classes where we'd burned art into panels of wood.

They didn't look inked at all. They looked like they had been branded into his skin.

"Stay away from me," I said, inching along the invisible wall. "I swear if you so much as touch me –"

"You'll what?" he said. "Tell daddy?"

He laughed at that and I had the distinct impression he was mad. Not stark raving crazy like I might imagine a regular psychopath would be, but an obsessive compulsive type with a touch of stand up comedian complex.

He levelled his gaze at me in a way that reminded me of someone pulling a mask down over his face. Like he didn't want me to see any emotion cross his features. As though he were trying to cut himself off from feeling anything.

I wasn't going to let him off easy. I had no intention of making killing me an easy thing for him. I was going to make it the most uncomfortable and guilt-inducing thing he'd ever done.

"I'm not even eighteen," I said as though that would make a difference. "I'm still a virgin for heaven's sake."

Not exactly my finest argument in light of the fact of the whole psychopath element, but it was out there now and I'd have to deal with it. If I was lucky, he would just be a regular murderous psychopath and not a sexual deviant as well.

"None of that matters," he said, and his tone was almost indulgent. "A few more lifetimes and you'll be closer than you are today. Just let all that go. I'm doing you a favor."

"A favor?" I blurted out. "You really are crazy."

Blessed raven feathers, holy oil, fire at all corners. Weird ritualistic tattoos. This was the stuff of insanity. It was the realm of psychotic breakdown.

"Seriously bat shit mad."

He eased himself around one of the puddles of glass as though he were averse to treading on it. I looked down at his feet. Bare. How ridiculous. Who came to a murder barefoot? I wondered if he'd done the same thing to Sarah. If she was tied up somewhere, gagged and terrified. Did he force her to text me? Was this one of those family members she had told me about?

"What have you done with Sarah?" I said. I had to know. If this was my last moment, I needed to know if she was alive or dead or waiting for me somewhere as afraid as I was.

He cocked his head at me. "Sarah? I don't know this human. Is she one of us?"

"One of us?" I heard a burble of ridiculous laughter make its way up my throat. "Look around you; we are human. We are going to burn because we are mortal, human bits of skin and flesh."

My voice broke on that last, and something crackled in

the depths of my memory. I expected him to leap at me. Instead, he cocked his head again, furrowed his brow.

"We aren't human," he said. "Not really. This is just skin."

He pulled at the flesh around his stomach as though it was a tight fitting shirt and I realized that talking was useless. Pleading, ludicrous. Even the sound of the fire crackling did nothing to sway his calm demeanor. My throat was burning from smoke, my lungs ached. I sucked in a breath, willing myself to stay calm. Cool. Say nothing. Just ease myself over to the nearest pew. I kept my eyes on him the whole time and let my hands roam the space around me. My fingers finally found the back of a pew and I pushed sideways in between the benches, inching along with my hands to find in the dark where the firelight couldn't reach. There were still some deep shadows in the cathedral even though the fire above me snapped and sizzled as it licked its way through the ancient wax and wood.

I took a quick look at the wall, searching for an exit that I hadn't thought of. Maybe one of the windows. Maybe I could climb up one of the statues and heave myself out one of those arched window panes devoid of their gorgeous stained glass.

I dared another look sideways toward the wall, hoping to see a gaping window frame somewhere nearby and discovered that the window closest to me was still intact. The fire from the galley lit up the colours on it in a magnificent way that would have made me gasp in awe if I wasn't so petrified.

I almost groaned out loud but managed to just clench my fingers on the bench. My breath came out in long hissing notes.

"What do you think about that panel?" he said. "Interesting, is it not?"

"Think?" I said, "You're planning to kill me and you want to know what I think about a stupid window?"

Three crosses. A skeleton helping a man down from the cross. Macabre, yes. Interesting, no.

By this time, the burning oil had begun to coat my throat and I started coughing. My lungs felt as though someone had reached inside and begun to squeeze them out like a wet rag. I was dragging in air, not breathing it. Every movement I made, shoving into the belly of the pew, grew harder.

I knew my knee was bleeding from where I had fallen on the glass. Fluid was trickling down my calf and pooling in my boots. Just thinking about it made me feel dizzy. I had to grip the back of the pew to keep from collapsing.

"You're failing," he said and shuffled closer.

I shook my head in denial. I would not let him win. I would not. Whatever was making me dizzy, it was nerves. Smoke inhalation. I could power through it. I had to.

"You think it's the smoke," he said, almost musing. "It's an easy mistake for a human to make. But really it's the oil. It's too powerful for us to withstand. Add blessed feathers to the equation--"

"Shut up," I yelled. His cool and calculating voice was

too much. Terrify me, torture me with threat of harm, but at least get out of my mind in the meantime.

Everything was shutting down and every word he spoke was as good as jamming splinters beneath my nails.

"You're having a hard time thinking," he said. "Aren't you? It's coming back, all of it. I knew it would."

"I told you to shut your mouth." I swayed backwards and fell onto the bench. I swore if I lost consciousness I was going to come back to it screaming and digging at whatever got in my way. I swiveled my head in his direction. I wondered whether or not I'd still be here in the morning when the firemen came or whether the psychopath would have lifted me from the bench and taken me God knows where.

"Leave me alone," I said. "I haven't done anything to you." My voice came out all scratchy and hoarse.

He reached the head of my pew and sat down on it. With an almost languid movement, he laid his arm across the back of the bench. His fingers were almost close enough to touch my shoulder. I shrank back, holding my breath. He looked even more terrifying up close. I knew I could throw a punch, but I imagined it would have no effect on that hard looking chin.

"Leave you alone?" he whispered. "You know I can't do that. You know, that in the end, you wouldn't want me to."

I watched, horrified, as he gripped the back of the pew and used it to pull himself the last few feet toward me.

It was happening. In seconds I was going to be beneath his grip and I had no idea what would happen to me then. I didn't even know if I'd be conscious enough to see it coming. I thought maybe it might be a blessing to pass out.

Somehow I found it within myself to fling myself onto the floor and claw my way underneath the bench, fishing myself back and forth to push myself deeper into the shadows. Dust went up my nose and coated my mouth. I could taste the oil in it. Not just Cyprus and Cedar wood. Something more holy than that. Frankincense. Again, I didn't want to think about how I would know such a thing. I couldn't afford to be even more scared.

I was scrabbling forward, pulling myself pew after pew through the church to the door. With each agonizing move forward, my knee ground into the floorboards and sent wave after wave of gritty pain up to my throat. The roar of fire had grown more distant as I dug my fingernails into the boards of the floor. Used them to yank myself forward.

I clutched something furry and cold and just managed to bite down on the scream that erupted up my throat, but couldn't keep myself from flinging the dead rat sideways in terror. Sweet Heaven, I couldn't breathe. Whatever air I had been dragging in before was now coming in short gasps. Everything was going black behind my vision.

I couldn't black out. I couldn't. I had to dig deep, pull my resolve together like the edges of a sweater. I thought I almost had a grip on the tattered thing when I felt his fingers around my left ankle.

I did scream then, letting loose the shriek that had been clotted in my throat with enough wind that I ended up sagging on the floor in exhaustion. At the same moment, he yanked me back toward him, and every inch of advance I'd made disappeared beneath my retreating fingertips until I ended up flipped over between pews, him leaning over me with one of those disgusting crow feathers in his hand.

"*Ligoria angelus*," he murmured and for a second, I thought I saw a tear running down his cheek.

"I'm sorry," he said as though he knew I had seen his tears.

I made a weak attempt to slap his hand away, but my arms felt as though lead weights had been tied to the wrists and before I could fend him off, the tip of the feather made a cross between my eyebrows. He was kneeling over me by then, and oil trickled down my temples and into my hair. I realized the sweat that was beading my forehead and running into my hair was more than likely tears. I was gagging on the sobs because I couldn't stop crying.

"Please don't hurt me," I heard myself saying. "I'm just a kid."

Everything that I'd ever done flashed before me. The year I had failed a grade because that was the year I'd gone into foster care. I ended up older than all of the other students. I thought I'd finally graduate this year. Go to university. Party it up. Put a distasteful past behind me. All that was washing away with that oil.

I gave him everything I had left in me with one hard jab of my knee and I didn't bother to wait to see if it was effective or not. Instead, as my knee pulled back into my stomach and caught him in the groin from the back, I threw myself onto my side and peeled myself out from beneath him. I was euphoric with the possibility of escape. Hope streaked through my chest the way a knife moves through liquid butter. I was out. I was clean. I just had to make it to the door.

I made it as far as the aisle before I realized that more debris had fallen from the gallery into the sanctuary and that the routes to freedom were few and far between. Fire lit up everything around me. I choked on my breath.

"You can't leave," he said from behind me. "You must know that."

"I don't," I said, protesting.

I gripped the leg of a pew bench and pulled myself to a staggering stand. Fire roared in my ears as I swayed on my feet. I craned to peer over my shoulder at him.

He was still terrifying. Broad chested with muscles in his neck thick enough to make it look like another man's thigh. And all over, covered in those black symbols that seem to come alive as the fire light danced over his skin.

I wouldn't give in. I couldn't.

"To Hell with you," I said.

He grinned. "I should hope not," he said. "Living on Earth has been hell enough."

I took a step backward. The back of my boot fetched up against that invisible wall again.

"Holy oil, sacred raven feathers, fire," he said, noticing my panic. "Don't you remember?"

I inched along the edges of the pews, deciding that if I

couldn't get out the regular way, I'd run for the altar. Even in a Gothic church, the priests never came in through the common entrance. There lay the way to escape. I almost laughed in relief to have remembered that other exit.

He was advancing on me just as slowly as I was inching away.

I almost slipped on the sandwich I had hurled at him earlier. My palm went to my stomach out of relief and instinct. That sandwich. I remembered making it. It was Sarah's favorite and I so wanted to help her. What kind of universe put a girl in a spot like this for wanting to be helpful?

Something in me sagged. Whatever it was, it finally stole everything from my muscles. I fell to my knees in the aisle. The blazing debris from the gallery snapping in my ears. As my hand went down, I felt a piece of glass slice into my palm, but I didn't even have the energy to cry out. Instead, I hung over my hands and knees watching the firelight play in the broken pieces of stained glass. Resigned, I fell backward onto my haunches.

Glass snapped beneath his step as he crept closer.

"That's it," he said. "It won't hurt. You'll be good as new tomorrow."

I braced myself for the feel of his fingers tangling in my hair. I might have even winced. But the pain in my scalp never came. Instead I heard him swear and in the next instant, he thudded onto his back just a foot away.

I blinked against the hot tears blurring my vision at the sight of him on the floor in front of me. I winced again from reflex as I imagined all of those shards of glass digging into his bare skin. My gaze caught sight of a smear of bread and banana next to him, and I realized in that second he had slipped on the sandwich. I laughed. I mean really laughed.

I should have run, but I didn't. Something rose in my chest to partner with the blind fear and I gave in to it.

I wasn't sure what happened next, I only knew that the shard of glass that was still in my hand rose above my head and came down onto his throat. I felt something hot spray across me and for a second, I thought it was more of that oil he had thrown at me earlier.

My mind was gone. There was only enough rational thought to tell me that I shouldn't be lifting my hand up one more time and bringing it down against his carotid. Whatever else might have made its way to my reason was lost as I swung for him again. I thought I heard him sobbing. It was only when I noticed he wasn't even breathing and the wailing sounds still echoed around the sanctuary that I realized it came from me.

I dropped the glass and fell to my palms over him.

Dead. He was dead and I was free. Giddiness drenched me. Remorse too. My stomach tried to heave itself up into my throat.

I sucked in the sobs. Swallowed them with a shuddering breath. My chest shuddered with the effort of collecting myself.

I pushed myself to my feet. The toe of my boot nudged his belly and I fought the rising bile. No use. I found myself quivering between the pews, retching up the spaghetti Gramp had made for supper.

When I pulled myself straight, a man stood in front of me. I suppose under normal circumstances, I would have shrieked and startled.

Circumstances were not normal.

"Who the hell are you," I demanded in the calmest, most of-course-there's-another-psychopath kind of voice. The crackling of the fire around me seemed almost surreal.

"You mean *what*," he said.

I was certain that I should be freaking out right then. With the fire crackling around me and this tattooed man at my feet, I should be screaming like a banshee.

Shock. So this is what it felt like. Numbness. I was aware I hadn't blinked, and I made a concerted effort to make my eyelids drop. He wavered for a second as my tear ducts tried to lubricate the movement.

"What, then?" I said to him.

"I am Azrael. The Angel of Death."

I blew air out of my mouth. Sure. Why not. The night was already past rational. I looked askance at the man who still lay on the floor, but now he was looking distinctly grey. Dead, definitely. I hitched in several shuddering breaths.

"You've come for him?"

He gave me a queer look that made me feel as though someone had reached into my throat and throttled my voice box.

"No," he murmured. "I came for you."

CHAPTER 3

I pushed myself to a stand, both hands gripping the back of the pew. I had no idea what was happening, but I wasn't going to let one more psychopath try to kill me.

"You see what coming for me got that guy." I gestured to the dead body, then I pulled up my fists like Sarah had taught me. I might have swayed a bit, but my fists were good and tight. Bewilder them with bravado if nothing else.

I was vaguely aware of the dizziness trying to overtake me, and that I was most definitely not steady on my feet. I knew I sounded weary and uncertain, and I was pretty sure that if he came at me, I wouldn't be able to do anything but glare at him. Even so, it was a matter of pride.

A specter of a smile twitched Azrael's lips but he never quite gave in to it. I waited, breath held for him to make his move, but he sighed instead and eased himself out of the pew and back into the aisle. I watched him stroll over to the dead man, a thin cane tapping the tiles with each step. It had a pointed silver tip that he used to nudge the dead man as he stood over him. Some relation, I thought, because the old man almost seemed to recognize him, though they didn't look remotely the same. The man on the floor was thick muscled and young. Azrael had a decrepit look to him even if he showed all the wiriness of a young man.

"He's dead," I said.

He swiveled his gaze back to mine. One silver brow cocked playfully.

"I see that," he said.

I stole a look at the gallery above me. Still burning, but not quite so fierce now. The other fires crackled almost playfully. If I made a run for it, I might be able to get halfway to the door before he even knew my intent.

"You won't get far," he said as though he had plucked the thought straight from my mind. Then his left hand shot into the air and his fingers snapped. Every single fire around me simply shut off as though by a valve.

"Holy crap," I said. "This can't be real."

I squeezed my eyes shut, putting every muscle of my face into the protest I would open them. And this would all be gone. The smell of guttered smoke, with all its musty undertones wafted my way.

"I can assure you I'm real," he said and I peeked one eye open, then the other. Nothing had changed except he stood there, watching me.

I felt rooted to the floor by that gaze. And when a glow rose in the sanctuary that seemed to come from nowhere and everywhere all at once, lighting every wrought iron sconce and chain, every wrinkled bit of plaster and fleck of aging gold paint, I had to lift a hand to shield my eyes.

"Not that I don't recommend running," he said. "Just that it isn't wise. At least not yet."

It was in that second that my calf muscle twitched and then spasmed. In the next second, a hot knife of pain burrowed through the tissues. I fell back onto the bench, gripping my calf with both hands.

"Holy Hell," I gasped out. "What did you do to me?"

By now the muscle in my calf wasn't just burning, it was twisting. I felt as though it was being torn apart and remolded. I couldn't do much more than hang over my knees and clutch the muscle, trying in vain to keep the pain in one place.

"The first one hurts a lot," he said. "Not that they don't all hurt, but since you're not expecting it this time.."

I glowered at him and said through clenched teeth, "The hell are you doing?"

He shrugged his shoulders and I realized for the first time he was wearing an immaculately pressed suit. In stark contrast, the shoes on his feet were worn out Birkenstock sandals snuggled tightly around red wool socks.

"I'm doing nothing to you," he said. "I promise you."

"Then what's happening?" I could barely get the words out through the pain. I ended up sucking in a breath and holding it, rocking back and forth in the pew as I tried to wait out the agony.

"You're being branded."

Three simple words but staggering in their implication. Branded. My thoughts flew to all of the marks on the psychopath. I could almost hear the cogs of my brain squeak as they worked out a connection between what was happening to me and the maniac on the floor. I realized that his marks hadn't been tattoos at all. Not one single one of them. I tried to consider how it would feel to have my eyelids branded like his had been, and something in me recoiled.

I lifted my head to peer over at him past this new, silver-haired threat's spindly legs. I caught sight of the inert body between them, and I could swear he was shrinking in front of my eyes. Was that glitter streaming out from his nostrils?

Like he had done with the psychopath, the man lifted his cane and pointed the tip of it at me.

"You'll get one of those for each fare you reap."

"Oh no," I said, gasping as another spasm worked his way through to the bone. "I don't know what you're talking about, but I don't want anything to do with it."

Azrael made a small circle in the air with the tip of his cane. "I wish I could say you had a choice."

"What are you talking about?" I ground out between clenched teeth. "What the hell is going on?"

Even before he could answer, the sparkling smoke emitting from the psychopath's nostrils started to gather above him. It was as though his body was disintegrating from the inside out and its particles were streaming out his nose into the air above him.

The dead man shrank as I watched and then he started to crumble to ash before it gathered into a plume of whirling dust. It funneled up into the glittery cloud and hung there suspended as though it were waiting for something.

I felt a strange tingling running over my skin and realized that the man's blood was lifting from each place it had splashed onto and was disintegrating into that same sparkling smoke. I watched it sail through the air from me to the same cloud.

"Holy Hannah," I murmured. This was too surreal. I had to be dreaming. I had to be, and yet the pain in my calf told me differently.

The old man gave his cane tip a sharp rap against the stone floor. With his free hand, he popped the top of the cane free and upended it, letting it lie in his palm. He eyed it for a moment with a thoughtful look on his face. It was unnerving to realize the handle he held was shaped like one of those grieving angels over a gravestone. It felt macabre even in the wash of what was going on around me.

With his other hand, he held open a leather pouch, dangling it from his fingertips so that the mouth of it was facing the cloud.

The glitter above where the dead man had been clenched into a ball midair and then streaked toward the opening of the pouch like a flock of starlings pirouetting through the sky. As each grain settled into the leather bag, he shook it, as though to ensure that everything would fit. A soft sucking sound came from the pouch as the last of the grains disappeared into its belly.

With a short grunt of satisfaction, he upended the pouch into the opening of his cane and then he popped the top back on and rested his hand atop it again, with his ring finger and pinky on one side of the wings and his thumb on the other, nestling his palm in the groove of the angel's back where the wings were spread. He peered at me over his cane with an expression of resignation.

"I've lost my mind," I murmured.

"Perhaps at one time," he said. Then he cocked that silver brow again as he pinned that penetrating gaze on me. "The pain is gone?"

I swallowed, assessing how I felt, and nodded. It was both a relief and a terror to know that.

"I thought so," he said and lifted the tip of his cane to point at me. A light streamed from it onto my leg and I couldn't help but pull my pant leg up to inspect the skin beneath.

I prayed there'd be nothing there, but of course there was. I had no idea what the symbol represented but it had been burned deep into my tissues so black that it left an echo of my pain on the skin. To normal eyes, I supposed it would look like a tattoo. But I had felt its inking as though it had come from my very blood and bone marrow. I would never be able to look at it without remembering the agony.

"You can run now," he said. "But I have a feeling you've changed your mind."

I pushed my pants back down over the mark and shook my foot.

"Damn straight I have," I said.

He tossed his cane up into the air and caught it in the middle then swaggered over toward me. If I'd thought him decrepit, his saunter with confident and almost powerful steps made me rethink it. I backed up with every step he took forward.

"Now, now," he said, a mother hen clucking at an errant chick. "I thought you weren't going to run."

"This isn't running," I said. I just didn't want him anywhere near me. He could tell me what he wanted to, what I needed to know, but after what I'd just seen, I would keep a safe distance from him.

"Semantics." He fluttered his fingers in the air. "So what is it you'd like to know?" he said.

"Maybe you can start with telling me what the hell this is." I waggled my foot at him as though he could still see a mark on my leg when I knew my pants covered it over perfectly.

"I thought I did," he said putting a finger to his chin. "Was I not clear?"

"About as clear as a bucket of tar."

He chuckled. "For every mystical being you reap, you get one of those. Just like he did. Until it covers every inch of your body."

I felt sick at that. "Every inch?" I tried to think of all

the tender areas of my body that I would rather not have poked with a needle let alone the burning pain that had run through my calf. I gripped my stomach without thinking and he seemed to notice.

"You'll get used to it," he said. "After all, there will be a lot of them before you're done."

"Done what?" I had backed away into the furthest pew I could find, thinking that I might turn tail and tear out of the place after all, push myself between those two drunken doors and hop on my scooter and be out of there. But the other part needed explanation, and I wasn't leaving until I got it.

He sighed as though he was losing patience. "Why do you think he was here?"

I let go a sound somewhere between disgust and confusion. I didn't want to think about that man. I didn't want to remember all of those markings. What did it matter? He was gone.

"Your guess is as good as mine," I said. "Catching some kind of psycho jollies. I suppose."

If he was upset about the description, he didn't show it. His face was a flat pond of water. Not a single ripple of expression.

"He was a reaper," he said.

"Yeah, right." I snorted. "Not like any Grim Reaper I've seen," I said, thinking about the hooded skeleton figure memes that flooded social media on occasion.

"You're right on that count," he said. "He was a different sort of reaper."

"What sort of reaper?"

"The kind that collects supernatural fares."

"Supernatural like vampires and werewolves?" I could hear the sarcasm in my voice, but if he did he didn't respond to it.

Instead, he nodded with a smile. "Exactly."

"So let me guess," I said. "He's been watching too many horror movies and thought I was some sort of nasty Nosferatu coming to drink someone's blood."

"Angel," he said.

"I thought you said he was a reaper."

He tapped his cane on the floor again. "Not him." His voice went sharp and firm. "You. You're the angel. Fallen, to be exact."

I wasn't sure what I expected, but it certainly wasn't that. I could accept that the psychopath believed he was doing some grim, supernatural task. I could even accept that this new threat believed he had some sort of otherworldly power. People went into asylums all the time because of stuff like that. Subtract from the equation the magical glitter due to hallucinations from smoke inhalation, and a girl got a full-blown, walking, talking delusion. But that didn't mean I was an angel. And it certainly didn't mean I was a fallen one.

A flush of heat washed over my skin.

"I think maybe I should call the police," I said, searching frantically for my cell phone.

"I wouldn't blame you," he said. "But they wouldn't answer anyway even if you could reach your phone."

He held his hand up, palm facing me, and in another second, my phone was just there. He closed his fingers around it and then tossed it to me.

"Perhaps you should sit down, Ayla," he said. "You look like you're going to pass out."

I did feel woozy. I let my hand roam around behind me until it found the bench. I sank down on it and slumped into the back. I felt even hotter now, as though the flames that he had put out earlier were still licking their way toward me.

"This isn't happening," I muttered. "I have to be dreaming."

"No dream." I felt him press into the bench with me and I smelled that same sugary aroma again, except this time it didn't smell burned. It smelled as though it had been pumped up with air into gossamer threads. His smell, I realized. I looked sideways at him. I had the crazy thought that beneath that old man facade, he might have been handsome once. There was such an earnest look on his face that I knew whatever was actual fact, this man believed what he believed. I peered over at the altar where the maniac had been. Of course, he wasn't there now. He was in the top of Azrael's cane. I almost giggled. Either the psychopath had never been there in the first place, or this was real.

I nodded at the top of Azrael's cane.

"So he thought I was some supernatural creature and was trying to reap me?"

"You *are* a supernatural creature," he said. "And that's

exactly what he was doing. Reaping a fallen angel was his last fare before he could collect his wings again."

I put my fingers to my temples to stave off the headache I felt tightening my scalp. Never mind that I had faced down a psychopath, killed a man, and just seen some impossible magic tricks--that last part was enough to make my skin hurt. My mind felt like it was going over the same track and couldn't jump out of its groove.

"So he's dead, then," I said, thinking about the psychopath who had attacked me. "Really dead?"

"Worse than dead," he said and tapped my lap with the top of his cane. "He's in here. In limbo."

Struggle as I would to process that information, I kept going back to the original issue. The reason the man was trying to kill me in the first place. I couldn't take my eyes off the top of that cane.

I sucked my teeth. "So limbo is real then?"

He nodded.

"Then God is a jerk if he thinks he can stuff souls into that little cane for eternity."

"That wasn't God's decision," he said. "It was the angelic host who decided that. And just for the record, regular mortals aren't trapped in limbo, at least not this kind of limbo."

He reached out and touched my shoulder. It was the merest, the smallest whisper of a touch, but it sent jolts of electricity all the way down to my toes.

"Only fallen angels end up like he did," he said. "But we can discuss that another time. What's before us now is your initiation."

I held my hands up in front of me. "No," I said. "Oh no. Just no. I don't care what you think you are or what you think this is, but I'm not getting involved."

I pushed to my feet and ran my hands along the backs of the pews to guide myself to the aisle. I was out of there. I didn't care what my hallucinating mind thought was happening. I planned to wake up in a few hours in my own bed and pretend that this was just a nightmare.

He appeared in front of me as though he had simply always been there and ran a hand over his silver hair, making it glitter much the same as the cloud I had witnessed earlier. It shivered for a moment and then turned into a long mane of lush black hair. He shook his head and it turned silver again.

"You seem to think you have a choice, when you already made it. Ages ago. Like it or not," he said. "You knew the risk of coming back with no memory, and now there's nothing you can do about what's happened. You're a fallen angel who has completed several hundred human incarnations. He was a fallen angel with all that to his credit and more. You killed him. Whether it was a conscious choice in this lifetime to do so or not, you are now a Nathelium. Simple."

"Doesn't sound so simple to me."

"I *am* oversimplifying a tad," he said. "It's not every fallen angel who gets the chance. Only after millennia of incarnations can you manage to even get to a grim reaper level. But it just so happens that you did spend a millennium reaping human souls. You just choose not to remember."

"Then why don't I have my god damn wings?" It wasn't just an accusation, it was a threat. I was about ready to collapse from shock and fury and none of this was making any sense. If it didn't make sense soon, I was going to turn all Dean Winchester on him.

He gave me a sad smile.

"You might have earned your wings," he said, looking back over his shoulder at the empty space where the dead man used to be. "But you failed just like he did. You had to start over. You would have remembered all of this if you had chosen to come back this time with your memories. But you always were stubborn. Just like you're refusing to believe now, you refused to do what was good for you then."

That was enough. Without thinking, I threw a punch, as hard a punch as I'd ever thrown. Rather than landing on anything, it simply thrust me forward and I fell onto the floor between the pews. I was scrabbling to find my balance and fell again. A ball of dust rolled onto my tongue and I coughed. Instead of dislodging it, all I ended up doing was inhaling more and I had to lie there for several minutes, trying to catch my breath and choke down dry dirt caked with old hair.

At one point, I looked up to see him peering over my head at me. His hair hung forward, tickling the tip of my nose.

"All better," he said.

I nodded, but I didn't feel all better. In fact, I felt all the worse, but I told myself that if he had come here to kill me, he would've done so by now. *Killing me.* The words rang like a bell on the back of my head.

"That maniac came here to reap me," I said and forced my gaze to his.

He cocked that silver eyebrow again. "Yes. I already told you so."

"That means I was supposed to die."

He smiled a knowing smile. "But you didn't."

"He said if I died, I'd come back as a human."

"Like I said: You might have if he had collected you. But he didn't."

I managed to roll over onto my side and he stepped to the left, leaning over the back of the pew to give me the space to get up. I squeezed my eyes closed. Like it or not, this was happening. And if it wasn't, then maybe the best thing was for me to just go along with it long enough to get out of there.

"Okay," I said. "You win."

He sighed. "This isn't a game," he said. "I assure you it's very real. Ozriel, the fallen one you just executed, was a Virtue before his fall. We all have certain roles, certain powers. Because you collected him, what was his is yours. To some degree, at least."

He inspected the tips of his nails and I got the feeling he wasn't telling me everything.

"What's the catch?"

He flicked his gaze to mine. "You always were astute,

Ayla."

"Just tell me."

"You can't go back to human reality," he said. "You look human, you breathe as a human. Your heart will beat the same as a human mortal's does. But at the end of your span, you will either have earned your wings and returned home, or you will come to me."

"Like my friend there," I said, guessing that the euphemism he used meant I would end up in the top of his cane as some glittering particles until the end of time. He didn't even bother to nod in agreement, but I knew I was right.

I thought of the poor maniac running me down like some robot with no choice and only one duty. Filled with tattoos that would have been agonizingly painful each time he was branded. I thought of the things he would've had to do, the creatures he would have had to face to get to this point. It seemed like a terrible penance. It seemed futile. I had the feeling the recovery of heavenly wings was a carrot being stretched out by a sanctimonious host who knew they had coated the bait in arsenic.

I set my jaw, bracing my back with my shoulders squared.

"Well I refuse," I said. "I don't care what you say or what you think is happening, but I have a choice. And I refuse."

"Angels don't have a choice," he said with a note of sympathy. "Only mortals do. That kind of thinking is what got you in trouble in the first place."

"I'll be sure to keep it in mind," I said. I was done with this conversation. It was time this entire night finished.

A slow smile threaded itself onto his mouth and for a moment he looked so staggeringly beautiful, I could barely take my eyes off him. He transformed again from an old man to a porcelain-skinned brunette with a glow around the edges of his body that for a second made it look like a large bonfire burned directly behind him and that he was only blocking a small bit of its light.

"Think what you will, Ayla," he said. "You can live out this allotted human life without reaping another supernatural soul, but at the end of it you will have no more incarnations, no more chances. This is it."

He pinned his gaze to mine, staring deep into my eyes as though he were looking straight through me to the back wall. I lifted my chin, defiant.

"Screw you," I said.

That full and soft looking mouth twitched and I got the feeling he was struggling to decide what words would come from it. I dared him with a cocked brow and he tossed me my cell phone. While I was busy grappling for the phone in midair, his gaze flicked upward and it wasn't until I had the thing securely between my hands I could follow his gaze.

"It seems the veil is lifting," he said, and I thought I heard the crackling of dry wood.

Oh horror of horrors, the gallery was still burning. All this time. Still burning.

Sweat trickled down my temple. I coughed on the thick

fingers of smoke that plunged down my throat.

I looked over at him, thinking to plead with him to at least stop the flames until I could get to the door, but he was gone.

And heaven help me if the fire he left was far stronger than the one he had shut down.

I pitched forward, throwing myself at the door, and in one single step, everything went black. I felt myself falling and even as I clutched for support, I thought it was too late.

Way too late.

CHAPTER 4

Someone was banging on a door somewhere. Glass shattered with a tinkling sound that seemed discordant in the echoes of the room. I heard several voices all at once and I believed for a second, I had somehow found my way into a crowded party where someone had the heat turned on too high and had burned whatever snacks they had stuck in the oven. It wasn't until I felt firm hands on my shoulders, shaking me that I remembered a person didn't go to a party and lie down on the floor for a nap unless there was something wrong. I remembered where I was when a set of gloved fingers peeled open my eyelids.

The cathedral. Fire.

I startled and tried to get up, but there were strong arms beneath my knees, preventing me from getting to my feet.

"I've got you," someone said. Someone used to being obeyed without question, obviously, because it had a stern quality of expectation to it. All the same, the voice might as well have been coming through water, it was so muffled. I fought him without meaning to. What if he was just some weirdo, trying to wrestle me into submission? I fired off a kick and contacted something hard. A shin maybe. He swore under his breath, but I heard it just the same.

"Relax." A command. Irritated this time, not happy to be ramrodded in the leg, probably, but trying to keep his temper. "This'll be easier if you let go."

"Screw you," I said because something about submitting made me both angry and terrified. I went limp anyway because the kick had taken everything out of me. I felt dizzy.

"I must be dead" I mumbled, and then I panicked because something else tried to worm its way through my mind. Something creepy. "Am I dead? Please God, tell me I'm still alive."

A quick image of a silver tipped cane flashed through my memory as I tried to slap his hands away.

"Which answer do you want?" he said, and his tone was brusque. Not sympathetic at all.

"Either, I guess," I mumbled, feeling stung. I was able to gauge the answer anyway, and they were both the same.

"You're one damn lucky girl," he said.

I tried to peer up at him as he crouched over me, but all I could make out was the blurry outline of a helmet. I blinked hard to rid my eyes of smoke and as my vision started to clear, I could make out the definite shape of a man. Yellowish helmet. Face Guard. Reflective tape pasted across the forehead.

Recognizing a fellow human being did not stop me from fighting his hands as they wrestled to cradle me against him. I had my pride, after all.

"I don't need saving," I complained and managed to roll from his arms onto my knees. I sagged back onto the floor and my cheek struck cold, dusty, smokey stone tiles. Grit embedded itself into my cheek. I think I sobbed in frustration.

He sighed, resigned.

"Okay, then," he said and tugged me onto my feet. He looked up at me through the visor as he crouched beside me. He still had a hold of my legs.

"You good?" He sounded as though he expected me to say no.

I nodded, still trying to blink my way to full awareness. When he let me go, I managed to stand perfectly still for all of three seconds before I started to crumple.

His snort said I told you so, and he caught me again before I fell. I ended up with my knees hanging from his elbow and my shoulders sagging against his arm.

I could see him shaking his head as he muttered something about me being like trying to save a drowning woman with a pocket full of rocks.

"I thought you all were supposed to be heroic, not nasty," I muttered and he hefted me into his arms a little too forcefully for my taste. Payback for my remark, I supposed.

I felt myself lifted into the air, high into the air because the thing that cradled me against its broad chest was a giant. I fancied I could feel his heart thrumming against my rib cage and it made something in my chest hurt.

"Get me out of here," I said.

He hitched me up higher still and my temple pressed into the soft part of his neck that was free of his gear. I thought I felt his pulse against my skin as he adjusted me in his arms, then I was moving in great strides down the aisle. There was a sort of safety in his arms that no doubt came from the relief of the stress I'd undergone. I snuggled in, content to let him carry me despite my earlier protests I didn't need saving.

The flurry of activity around me sort of parted like the Red Sea for Moses and I realized it was comprised of firemen fighting the blaze, doing their best to save what was left of the landmark church even if it was a derelict. No doubt they worried for the buildings around it and the squat bungalows that housed families who had lived in Dyre for generations. I gave a brief thought to them as well, but it wasn't quite as nice. I wanted to know why none of them had come to my aid while I'd been staggering around in there, choking on smoke and hallucinating psychopaths and murder by glass shards.

The hiss of water and foam striking flames came to me through the murk of sound and I thought I could hear breathing apparatus sucking for smoke-filled atmosphere and filtering it into clean air.

I squeezed my eyelids closed again, reveling in the feel of the tears that cleared my eyes of smoke. I was alive. I never thought I would enjoy so much the feel of cold air striking my cheeks as my savior scuffed out onto the stone steps. I sucked in fresh air and immediately coughed up half a lung.

"Just stay calm," he said. "We'll get you oxygen. That will make it easier to breathe."

I heard each steady step as he ran down the stone staircase to the asphalt. Red lights blinked into the darkness around me. It felt as though there was a throng of people pressing in, peering over his shoulder to look at me. I saw several faces, mouths working as though in pity. Swallowing felt like glass was digging into my throat. I wondered which face, if any, was my grandfather's. Then I realized something else, something that made me struggle against the mask that was pressing to my nose.

I had come to save Sarah and had ended up stuck inside the burning building. Hallucinating until I finally passed out as I tried to escape the flames.

"Sarah," I blurted out, swiping at his hand. "She's still in there."

The roughness of his glove then as he pressed his hand onto mine, holding the mask in place, was nothing compared to the way he shoved me onto the stretcher on my back. He still had hold of my head as he cradled it in one hand and the mask pressed to my face with the other. There was a growl in his voice when he spoke.

"You mean there's someone else in there?"

I nodded as best I could with the back of my head pinned against his palm and my nose stuffed into a plastic mask. I thought I heard him curse, but he was already yanking his hand out from beneath my head. I grappled for his cuff. For some reason, I didn't want him to leave me. Even if Sarah was still in there. I had an irrational fear that Azrael would return, and I'd be swimming beneath all of that fear again.

He turned to me with something like compassion in his eyes and the contrast of it to earlier made my eyes water.

"You'll be okay," he said through the breathing apparatus. His voice sounded hollow and I tried to yank him closer, to keep him from leaving me.

"Really," he said, peeling my hands from his collar. "You're in good hands." He whirled around, and I heard him hollering that there was someone else inside.

I was left to the ministrations of a paramedic who checked my vitals and peered beneath my eyelids. A blood pressure cuff got wrapped around my bicep and someone threw a silvery blanket over me. I knew there was only one ambulance in all of Dyre so I doubted it would take off without Sarah if they found her. I just had to wait. I'd done what I could for her.

The kindly paramedic didn't ask me too many questions that didn't have anything to do with how I felt. Thankfully, he didn't care what had brought me to the cathedral and he didn't care whether or not I believed I had seen angels, ghosts, or demons in there. He just cared my heart rate was normal for someone under a great deal of stress and that there was plenty of oxygen in my lungs.

Eventually, he let me sit up on the back of the ambulance step, wrapped in the silver blanket because he couldn't find anything terribly wrong with me that rest and warmth wouldn't fix.

I almost laughed at that. I had my doubts whether either one of them would fix my fear that I hadn't been hallucinating at all. I didn't dare touch my calf, for fear it would confirm my suspicions. I elected instead to watch the firefighters get control of the blaze that was all too real. They made noises that I understood. They yelled to each other. The bystanders milled about, whispering about tearing the building down. The stink of smoke made sense. So, too, did the swiftly decreasing licks of flame that had begun to chew away at the rooftop.

Through it all, I waited anxiously to see my rescuer carrying out a second form, and it took what seemed like forever before he exited. The fire seemed to be under control by then, if not out, and as he trotted out onto the stone steps, he pulled his helmet from his head, shaking free a mat of tar-coloured hair. He was indeed tall, at least six foot four, perhaps three years or so older than me. His gloves went beneath his armpits, and he raked his fingers over his scalp, making the hair stand on end. He looked sooty and sweaty and confused.

But he was not carrying anyone else.

"Looks like they didn't find anyone else," the paramedic said to me. "Are you sure there was someone in there?"

I chewed my lip. What could I say except the truth.

"Not really." I fumbled for my cell phone, hoping that before I'd fallen unconscious, I'd thought to ram it in my pocket. I groaned out loud when I realized it was probably still in there on the floor somewhere because it was not on me anywhere.

"I had a text from a friend," I mumbled. "She said she was here."

He made a noncommittal sound and bent to check the blot of blood on my pant leg where I'd cut myself with the glass. I twitched my leg away.

"It's nothing," I said because I didn't want to even see what might be beneath my pants. He shrugged and by that time my fireman had strode over to the ambulance. He was holding out something in his clenched fist.

"This yours?" he said.

"My cell phone," I said, relieved. "See?" I said to the paramedic. "I'll show you."

"Whatever it is," the fireman said. "It can wait. There's more pressing things right now."

I lifted my gaze to a set of piercing eyes that must have been the colour of jade in the light of day. I shook my cell phone at him, assuming he'd understand by my obvious sense of urgency that I grasped the direness of the situation.

"That's what I'm trying to tell you," I said.

He seemed unimpressed by my sincerity.

"Who do you think was in the building?" he demanded. "We didn't find anyone in there. Nothing. No one. Just your phone."

"You searched everywhere?" I asked. "Are you sure? I have a text from her. I'm telling you, she told me to meet her here."

He watched me with a sort of detached attention, and I had the feeling he was examining me. He didn't believe me, that was clear. Something else was going on behind that penetrating gaze of his. I had the distinct impression he thought I was guilty of something. I had a feeling I knew exactly what it was. I had seen that look before.

"What were you doing in the building?" he said.

I lifted my chin, stubborn. "I already told you. I came to help a friend."

His hand snaked out for mine before I could react and his fingers found the pulse on my wrist.

"You checked her over?" he asked the paramedic. "She's not delirious?"

"I most definitely am not delirious," I snapped. I had to smother down the retort that I might have been an hour earlier, but he didn't need to know that. "My friend Sarah was supposed to be in there," I said. "She texted me." I pressed the revive button on my cell phone, thinking I could swipe to the text messages and show him. "She was the one that said to meet her here."

The phone refused to turn on. Dead. Great. Just when I needed the thing.

The fireman swung an accusing glare to me.

"If she's alright," he said to the paramedic. "Then she can tell me what she was doing in that church in the middle of the night."

I cursed without caring who heard me. The paramedic's eyes went wide in surprise. No doubt he expected a regular teenager's caution around adults. Well, I was close to escaping teenage years and now that I'd just been through hell, I wasn't going to let anyone bully me, let alone a guy that looked suspiciously close to my own age even if he was wearing full fireman regalia.

"I didn't set the fire," I said. "If that's what you're thinking." I shoved the blank phone in his face. "She texted me. I can prove it."

"We searched everywhere," the fireman said and dropped my hand onto my lap. He turned those eyes onto the paramedic and I watched his jaw clench as he obviously tried to assess whether or not I was too far in shock to understand reality without letting on to me that was exactly what he thought.

"At least the fire is out," he said. "If anyone was in there, they're gone now."

I sighed and pulled my arms around my waist, tucking the blanket in between the crook of my arm and my midriff. If that was the case, and Sarah really was gone then all I wanted to do was get home. Maybe if I charged up my phone, I could return the text and see if she got back to me. The girl didn't just disappear for years and then text out of the blue for no reason.

"My grandfather is probably wondering where I am," I said. I tried to push myself off the back of the ambulance and onto my feet with every intention of heading to my scooter, but my descent was a little clumsy and I ended up grabbing for his arm to steady myself.

He held me by the waist until I found my balance. His palm felt too hot for comfort. It made me think of fire and smoke and it sent an uncomfortable ache along the column of my throat. I could barely swallow for heaven's sake. And there was a weird zinging feeling running down my spine.

Thankfully, he pulled his hand away so I could find some semblance of calm again, but he leveled me with a direct, green-eyed stare.

"Where are you going?"

I nodded at my scooter, where it still sat at the bottom of the steps. It seemed an eternity ago I'd rumbled through the streets on it bound for this church.

"Home."

He shook his head. "You're not driving that. Not in your condition."

He lifted his gaze as though he were searching for something. "My car is over there." He jerked his chin in the direction of the crowd and I noticed a dark little beat up GTI.

He tucked the blanket around me. "I'll take you home and I'll get one of the volunteers with the truck to follow behind with your scooter."

"I can manage," I said.

I didn't want to say that the way that he was bustling about as though he owned the place, presuming things about me that weren't true, the least of which was acting as though I was some kid, was a real big turnoff.

In the end, he did find someone to hoist my scooter up

into the back of a truck. I shoved into the passenger side of his car and stared out the window, stubbornly refusing to look at him or talk to him as he buckled up. Quite the little safety officer, apparently. He thought I was an arsonist, that much was clear. I gave him clipped directions on how to find my house and sank into the back of the seat, deciding to wait out the ten minutes it would take to travel across town.

"I can charge your phone if you like," he said, breaking the silence as he turned the key. Whether he was looking at me when he did so or straight out of the windshield, I wouldn't know. I just kept staring out my side.

There was a nasty rumble coming from beneath us as the car sputtered to life.

"I'm Callum," he said.

"I'm unimpressed," I answered. I had met his kind before. Dazzle me with kindness. Think a little bit of pretend camaraderie would make me divulge all my truths. Fat chance of that.

"We have the same phone," he said, sounding almost apologetic. "You can use my charger."

My fingers were clenching and unclenching over my lap. He didn't fool me. I knew what he was trying to do.

I peered sideways at him. "It won't be charged in time for you to see I was telling the truth, so thank you but no."

I noticed the knuckles of his hand on the steering wheel went white.

"Thought so," I snorted and then turned back to the window.

I expected him to try again like most folks did. I almost wished for it.

"Suit yourself," he said, the apologetic tone completely gone.

Well, good. Nobody liked a pretender anyway.

Clusters of bystanders had begun to break apart from the larger horde of looky-loos. One woman with two small children started tapping onto her cell phone and only narrowly missed one of them running in front of our car. She snagged the little fellow just in time and looked sheepish beneath the glower Callum gave her from behind the steering wheel.

So I guessed I wasn't the only one he drilled with that nasty look. Maybe I shouldn't feel so special about his abrasive attitude toward me. Even so, I sat on my side, a sullen presence next to what felt like a tightly wound gear over the next few minutes. He drove in silence.

He pulled up in front of my house. The porch light was on over the front step, emitting a soft and comforting glow. In contrast, the kitchen light was also blazing, but that left me with an entirely different feeling. My grandfather was up. He was waiting.

Callum parked neatly beside the curb and cut the engine.

"You don't have to come in," I said, panicking.

He swung that green gaze to mine. "Your scooter," was all he said, but he delivered the line with a cocked eyebrow that indicated he thought I was stupid. I must have been, too, because I couldn't fathom what he meant by it.

"My scooter? What about it?"

"Charles will need some help getting the thing off the back of his truck."

"Oh," I said. "Right." I fumbled for the latch but the door wouldn't open. I had the awful urge to pinch the bridge of my nose in exasperation.

"Sticks sometimes," he said, reaching across the seat and gripping the handle over the backs of my fingers. I sucked in a breath as his palm brushed across my skin. A kaleidoscope of images reeled about behind my eyes, leaving me dizzy and cringing backward into the seat. I couldn't move as he pulled his hand back as the door clunked open, then reclaimed his position on his side of the car.

He gave me a look that seemed almost concerned. "Sure you're alright?" he said.

He looked at me, waiting as I sat gawking openly at him. I had to blink him back into focus through the remnants of those awful images, the feeling that I was still back in the church.

I finally managed a nod. Two quick waggles of my chin as the light in the car winked on. There. That seemed normal. I hoped.

"Well, okay, then," he said. "You're good to go."

"Good to go," I echoed, hoping I looked less shell shocked than I sounded because whether I believed what happened in the church had been a hallucination or truth, there was one thing I knew right then. Something wasn't right about his touch. Not right at all. And my impression of why it didn't feel right had just one explanation. It simply didn't feel human.

CHAPTER 5

I couldn't get out of the car fast enough to be honest, and if I slammed the door behind me, it was only because I wanted out of there as fast as my little legs would take me. I certainly wasn't trying to draw attention to my exit. Not at all. The faster I got out of there without any notice from him, the better off I'd be. Who wanted to be stuck in an inhuman thing's memory after all? Not this chick.

Even so, I felt his eyes on me as I speed-walked to the door, trying to be all nonchalant about it and knowing I wasn't successful. I lurched more than strolled, and my knee felt swollen and clunky, making my progress an agonizingly slow one.

I stood on the step with one hand on the knob and the other one clutching my cell phone. Just in case. I had the discomforting thought that Sarah might have been inside the church after all, and that Callum had found her and lied about it.

My fingers squeezed the door handle. I knew how I sounded to myself. Paranoid. That had to be a good sign, didn't it? You only sounded crazy to yourself if you were in your right mind, right? Surely if you had really gone mad, you wouldn't be thinking you sounded crazy.

But I couldn't stop thinking that maybe Callum was partners with that psychopath and had tied her up down there, waiting for the chance to return and feed whatever sick desires had set them on an innocent girl in the first place.

My mind stopped short of imagining what those desires might be. I'd had enough trauma for one night. But thinking about the maniac I'd encountered made my knees shake again. Because there had been a psychopath, hadn't there? I'd killed him.

My fingers spasmed on the metal as I recalled it. I sent a cursory glance down at my clothes, almost expecting them to be filled with blood. Of course, they weren't. Either it had been syphoned off by Azrael or it had never been there in the first place. I swept those thoughts abruptly under a rug in the darker drawers of my mind. I was jittery. That was all. There had been no maniac. No strange smell of fragrant oils or feathers falling from heaven. Just fire and smoke and terror enough to make me hallucinate.

I took a deep breath to calm myself and brace myself for going in. Just get inside and charge my phone and shoot a text off to Sarah. Things would sort themselves out from there. She would no doubt text me back, growling at me a little bit for abandoning her, and I would growl at her for being so cryptic, and then we would send cute smiley icons to each other, relieved we were both fine.

A good night's sleep was all I needed. Just because I had imagined some maniac in the church didn't mean she had been attacked by one. Didn't mean Callum was a maniac. The old Sherlock Holmes rationale that the simplest explanation was probably the correct one was no doubt the right explanation. She'd waited for me and when I hadn't shown, she had left. Or when the fire started, she had left. Or she'd never been there in the first place. No matter which scenario was correct, she was not still there. I repeated it to myself as I stood there on the step.

"Not there, Ayla," I said and felt better just hearing my voice. "Let it go."

I clung to each explanation as I braced myself to push the door open. And it was only as I began to calm down that I realized things weren't quiet inside my house. Sounds of muted conversation came from inside. Gramp was most definitely not alone as he waited for me.

"Crap," I muttered. Surrounded front and back. I almost wanted to peek over my shoulder to see if Callum was still sitting in his car, waiting. I resisted. Barely.

Gramp obviously had been contacted by some Good Samaritan neighbor who thought 1:30 AM was a decent hour to come calling and warn a man his granddaughter had come ever so close to burning to death in an abandoned church. I chewed my bottom lip. No doubt he was worried since I hadn't called. No doubt when he saw me perfectly safe and alive he would have his typical relieved hissy fit because his first instinct after fear was anger. Strange thing for a self-professed druid, but we can't all be perfect.

Despite the druid in him wanting to be progressive, the grandfather in him worried about me constantly.

I considered simply turning back around and waiting somewhere until the old ladies were gone and face Gramp alone. Maybe it might even be smart to slip around back and go up the back way to my bedroom. It was an old house, so there were still servant's stairs winding up a narrow path to the back of the building. I might have considered it if not for the brooding guy in the car behind me with his bead on my head like a sniper's rifle.

I shot a look over my shoulder, checking to see if Callum was still there in his car. He was. The light was on inside, and he was gripping his steering wheel with both hands as he leaned forward for a better look at me. I told myself that if he really was inhuman and wanted me dead, he would have taken the opportunity to end me while I was in the car. He was just a guy waiting to be sure his fare made it home safe.

Or he wanted to be sure I went in and didn't find my way back to the church.

I shot him a feeble smile, testing to see if he really did have a clear sight of my face. He lifted his hand off the steering wheel in salute but his expression didn't change. It still held that suspicious look. It seemed I was stuck here in limbo until either the truck arrived and he could help get my scooter off the back, or I gave in and went inside to face the music.

"Come on," I said through a grit-edged smile, my teeth clenched together, and I wasn't sure whether I was trying to convince myself to go inside or coax the universe to send the truck in rapid delivery of my scooter so that I could rid myself of the unnerving presence in the car.

I sighed with relief when the pickup truck he had commandeered along with its driver, who I presumed was Charles, pulled up behind him. Charles was a burly sort of man. Short and squat. He hollered to Callum who broke into a smile for the first time since I'd met him. My mouth twitched at that. If he was an inhuman thing, I had to admit he was a handsome one with that smile. Maybe even incredibly handsome. Maybe something like gorgeous.

I watched, fingers clenched around my cell phone as they grunted Old Yeller out of the back and rolled it up my driveway.

Callum shot me a look as he tapped the scooter's seat, daring me to hop back on it and grinning because he knew I wouldn't. Not with him there, anyway. Charles lifted his hand in a wave then ran for his truck and pushed behind the wheel. I was surprised at how much energy he had after fighting the blaze in the church, but he roared off in seconds, leaving Callum and I standing there, facing each other.

"Are you all right?" he said, strolling toward me as though he expected me to invite him in. "You look kind of off."

I swallowed down hard. In the full porch light, I knew he could see every move I made. No doubt he could see every expression cross my face. I could see him pretty clearly from where I was. That black hair of his stuck up in the back as though he had been running his hand through it. His eyes were rimmed with exhaustion.

He looked human.

"I'm fine," I said. "Just a little scared." It was true, actually. Even my pulse agreed.

I could swear his whole body softened then. "I can come in with you," he said. "If you like."

I nearly jumped out of my skin at the brash hint for an invitation.

"You're not a vampire, are you," I said, without thinking, then when he gave me a cocked eyebrow for a response, I realized how ridiculous I really sounded. I was glad of it, actually. Saying the thing out loud made it seem less possible.

"Never mind," I said. "I'm good. It's all good." In an effort to put a stop to the way my head had started waggling up and down, I swung around and pushed the door open.

The lights inside nearly blinded me. I had to shield my eyes with an uplifted palm. Whatever mutterings of conversation had reached me through the door were nothing to the arguments going on within.

All I could make out through my fingers at first was the cheesy velvet patterned wallpaper and the row of school pictures of my mother that led like bread crumbs up the stairs. I knew the picture of her in her wedding gown was furthest along the firing line, and I did what I always did when I came in the house. I flicked my gaze away from that row of smiling faces because it seemed creepy somehow, except this time I was greeted by more faces. Faces with hostile eyes that met my fidgety gaze with every bit of malice I had just faced back at the cathedral. At least these were no otherworldly monsters. These three very prim looking neighborhood ladies were monsters from my own realm, lined up in the hallway as though they were at a complaint department.

"There she is," Mrs. Vanda said. An accusation I met with bravado before hunching over to see if I could catch sight of Gramp somewhere on the other side of the sea of old women.

"Gramp?" I said, and was a little irritated at myself for the way the enquiry came out like I was some frightened kid. I cleared my throat to remind myself I was not a kid. This was not four years ago when I didn't know these women and I quailed at the thought that they might be angry at me. I casually picked up one of the shells that sat amidst the hundred or so wooden trinkets Gramp had amassed and piled upon the telephone table at the bottom of the stairs. There. I felt more settled.

I looked around the women as though they weren't there. "Gramp, where are you?," I called out. "What's going on?"

"Ayla." A movement from the corner of my eye. I followed it to where he stood somewhere past the hags, and it took a moment before I noticed him waiting fully dressed on the other side of the pass through counter between the living room and the hallway. He used it as a sort of pharmacy counter for the hippies who came for his salves and ointments. I secretly believed he sold pot on the side, but I would never accuse him of that. He was in his 70s, for heaven's sake.

At the moment, he was using that pass through counter as a sort of barrier between him and the harridans of the street who had tormented me for the entire four years I'd lived here. Blamed me for all sorts of nasty incidents: graffiti on their trash cans, setting fire to paper bags on their steps when I was past that kind of juvenile behavior by the time I arrived. I shouldn't have been surprised to see them here at this time of the night, blaming me again for something that had nearly killed me.

"Tell them," Gramp said. He had a tight look to his lips that surprised me. I expected him to be more supportive of me and less indulgent of those nasty neighbors.

I did a double take. "Tell them what?"

"Tell these women you didn't set that fire," he said.

"Of course I didn't," I said and dropped the shell down onto the counter.

Mrs. Vanda snorted.

"Well, I didn't," I said, facing her with a glare. The curlers in her hair were a hot pink that made the purple rinse in her hair seem clownish.

Gramp disappeared from behind his pass through window for a moment and then reappeared in the doorway at the end of the hall. He stood there at the entrance to the kitchen with his garden browned hands on his hips. I understood that posture all too well. I'd seen it plenty.

"You think I did it," I said. It wasn't surprising that he thought so, but it did hurt. "Don't you?"

He scuffed his feet on the ageing gold shag carpet. I noticed he was wearing his Birkenstocks and for a second, a silver-haired man in red wool socks and sandals flashed across my mind. I couldn't breathe as the image pulsed there like a fevered artery behind my eyelids. I had to reach out to the wall to fight off the dizziness.

It wasn't until I felt the back of Gramp's fingers against my forehead that I realized I had all but blacked out.

I blinked up at him. He was tall for an old man. Still wiry and thick from his daily yoga practise and penchant for spinach smoothies. His bushy grey eyebrows furrowed together to meet above his eyes. They were black and every bit as piercing as a hot needle. I think my chin quivered. No doubt my reaction looked like guilt at that moment.

"Are you all right?" he said. "What happened? You're not on something are you?"

It was his tone that did it. I might have cried, but instead I felt a flush of anger.

"Of course I'm all right," I said. "Why wouldn't I be, when I just almost burned to death." I almost choked on that last, because I wanted to lash out at him about his drug comment, but I just couldn't get it out.

I expected him to gasp at that horrific news, but of course, word had come ahead of me, and he had already processed the fact I'd been stuck in a burning building and had moved to why that building was on fire in the first place. That was when he looked me up and down for what I guessed was the first time since I'd entered and saw something other than the granddaughter he expected to be filled with soot and sweat and tweaking pupils.

He reached down to pinch the material of my pants at the knee. Inspecting it, he twisted it back and forth. I looked down at the way his hands inspected my pants. Of course, the maniac's blood was gone. If it had ever been there, and the proof of that was the way he only worried the pants at the knee, where my blood soaked through.

"You hurt yourself," was what he said. Compassionate but cautious. Mrs. Vanda sent another scorching comment my way and he looked back over his shoulder at her. I could only guess what it must've been by the way she clamped her lips closed.

His palm went beneath my chin, his fingers gripping the back of my neck. This time more tender. His natural empathy was flooding to the surface, but it was cautious. I had the feeling he was checking for some residual high but wanted it to look like he was just concerned.

Those black eyes of his bore into me. Years ago, I might have squirmed.

"What happened?" he said.

Everything was on the top of my tongue and ready to spill out: the text from Sarah, slipping out and driving to the church, the smell of smoke and soot and fire. I was still struggling to understand the hallucinations and what they meant.

I started to put the experience into words, knowing he would listen, but one of the women whispered something about me being high as a kite to Mrs. Vanda and the moment was gone. My eyes flicked to the women behind him.

I backed away from the door and found the steps with the back of my boots.

"I'm going to my room," I said. It felt very much like something a young teenager would say, and I resented I had to use that tactic. But it was the best I could do with them all staring at me. I felt as though even breathing had become difficult. The adrenaline soaking my tissues had started to shut down my mind and what was left was urging me to run out the door and up the street until I couldn't run anymore.

"Wait right there," Gramp said with his palm in the air. "I'm not letting you off that easy this time."

"I'm eighteen for heaven sake," I argued. I couldn't stay there. Not with those women and their accusing eyes. "You can't stop me from going to my room."

"In six months," he said, correcting me. "And until then, I have every right."

It had nothing to do with rights, but I couldn't say that to him with them standing there watching every movement.

Mrs. Vanda took a step forward, as though she wanted to assert herself. "I'm telling you, she's a demon," she said. "She set that fire sure as shooting."

There it was. Flat out. That thing they were all thinking. What Callum had thought. What Gramp was thinking now. Something in my stomach hurt. I could barely lift my gaze to look at him.

The look on Gramp's face as he took in the woman made me think for a second that he might forgo his gentle and peaceful nature. Rip her a new one. Instead, I watched as he inhaled very deeply, obviously gathering his self-control from the corks of his Birkenstocks. I waited for him to speak, and when he didn't, I clenched the banister.

"If I was going to burn the place down," I said. "Do you really think I'd be stupid enough to do it while I was still inside?"

She shrugged. "You've done stupid things before."

I wanted to scratch her eyes out right then. Gramp stepped in front of her just as I lurched forward with every intention of doing just that. I caught his eye and realized his entire expression had softened. Those black eyes of his pinned themselves to my gaze and I knew looking at him that he knew-- just knew--I was at my limit. I halted as though he had gripped me by the shoulders.

Without so much as turning around, he lifted his hand in the air much the way an army marshal might to calm a crowd of unruly protesters. His eyes never left mine as he told them all to quiet down and go home. My gaze flicked past his shoulder to Mrs. Vanda. Her lips twisted into a tight line. Even so, she wrapped her coat around her shoulders, gathering her dignity. I had to resist the urge to stick my tongue out at her. And it was only because I was too busy clamping down on the sobs that wanted to escape.

She might have actually left and allowed me to breathe again, but a sharp rap sounded on the door and I jumped onto the bottom tread of the stairwell, my fingers spasming around the banister.

I could see Callum's dark head through the mottled window. I shuddered as I remembered touching him and feeling that terrible and ludicrous sense that whatever he called himself, Callum, Fireman, or hero, he was not human.

CHAPTER 6

Panic settled around my shoulders like a heavy coat.

"Don't open it," I said. Even I could hear the shrill note in my voice and I thought a splinter dug into my finger from the banister as I clutched at it.

I couldn't wait for him to come in or for the women to leave. I needed escape. I fled up the stairs and went straight to my room where I could slam the door just like a spoiled child. I didn't care that it felt good and that, at my age, I shouldn't have enjoyed it, I just did. I headed to the charger on my bureau and plugged in my phone. Twenty minutes. That was all it would take to get to at least half a charge. I could probably check it again in five.

I tried not to listen to what they were saying as I waited for my phone to charge, but it was tough. My bedroom was at the top of the stairs and the women at times were shrill as they decided to recite every last thing I had done to their properties during my first years in Dyre.

What they didn't understand was that then I was troubled and grieving and angry and scared. I'd been acting out. Just like most kids that age, and in that situation. Gramp had taken me in and stood up for me when no one else would.

The problem with that was I wasn't ready to be normal. I wasn't ready to be loved. It had taken my grandfather months upon months to build up a trust that allowed for an uneasy sort of truce where I left the house for school on my own in the morning even if I did avoid contact with every normal-looking teenager I could. I went out in the evening past curfew to meet up with some of the more nefarious dropouts who hung around in musty basements. He didn't ask me how my days at school went and I didn't tell him about the things I did in those musty basements. It was all part of the trust building process. And I tested that trust. Oh, how I had tested it, time and again, trying to force him to give up on me.

But he hadn't. And I loved him for it so fiercely, I would die for him.

So if those old women were honest with themselves, they would know I hadn't set a single fire in at least a year.

Every now and then I heard Callum's voice as he tried to reason with them. I wondered what he wanted from me, why he was in my house at all, defending me to women who would never see me as anything other than a delinquent.

Just as curious was the way my grandfather was deferring to him, even going so far as to agree with Callum when he said things like arsonists always returned to the scene of the crime, but are rarely foolish enough to be inside when they set the place to light. So. It seemed Callum either believed me or wanted something from me.

No doubt he wanted something from me. A person didn't just defend someone they didn't know for no reason. No matter how pathetic they looked. I didn't care how kind and compassionate he acted. In my experience, that was a sure sign someone wanted something from me.

I crossed my arms and leaned against the door, straining to hear. Maybe they'd just all go away. I knew Gramp was too polite to ask them to leave, but I also knew he wanted more than anything to talk to me about what had gone on in the building. He wanted to believe me; I knew he did because he always wanted to believe me. But this time, with one of the town's landmarks nearly destroyed, he would need more of an explanation. Like why I was in there in the first place.

I had nothing to be ashamed or afraid of. And now, safely in my room, with the familiarity of the smells of the house around me and the warmth of the furnace pumping quietly through the grates, I began to relax. See things for what they really were. Everything had been just a horrible nightmare. The fire had been real, certainly, and my near death of asphyxiation too. But the rest of it? The maniac, the Angel of Death, the feeling like Callum wasn't really human. All figments of an overactive imagination. Foolishness born of fear and exhaustion, not drugs like they all wanted to believe.

I blew relief out between pursed lips and looked around to be really sure I was home. I had never truly made the room my own in the four years I'd been here. It was still strewn with the books and papers that my grandfather had accumulated over his lifetime. This had been his office at some point, and if I looked beneath the facade of jeans and dresses and shoes littered over the space, I could still see all of the things that he'd left.

Eventually, I heard the women move into the hallway and out onto the porch. I heard Gramp tell them he would look into it and that everything would be alright.

I wanted to believe it. I think even Callum did, because I could hear him asking Gramp what he was going to do.

"Believe her," he said and my heart warmed just hearing it. One stalwart champion in a town of enemies.

"She said she was there to see a friend," Callum said.

I could almost hear Gramp shrug as he answered. "If she says so, it must be true, but I can't imagine it would be." He sighed loud enough for me to hear all the way up the stairs. "Whatever people she hangs out with on occasion, she would never call friends. She's been such a wild thing."

"Trouble, huh?" Callum said.

"Like a terrified squirrel except one that attacks you instead of running away," Gramp said with a laugh. "Do you know I had to buy a new bed for her when she came? She refused to sleep in her mother's room, and I figured out pretty early it was because she wanted me to think she could leave at any time. So I just let her stay in my office. It was just easier that way. Didn't even bother to move the bed from her mother's room in there. I figured after a while she wouldn't be so threatened by kindness and would eventually move into her mother's room."

"Did she?" Callum asked.

"What do you think?"

It was disconcerting to hear the struggles I had put Gramp through when I'd first come summarized into so few words, but I supposed it was accurate.

Poor Gramp. He had put up with so much from me.

I sagged against the door. I was exhausted and I wanted nothing more than to climb into bed and fall asleep, but I knew Callum would leave and Gramp would be turning down the lights and coming upstairs to bed. I expected him to stop at my room. I stole a look at my phone, just in case. If it was charged enough to turn it on, I could show him the texts from Sarah and at least prove she existed.

The charger light was on but nothing flickered to indicate a message of any sort. I shouldn't have been surprised. The only people who ever contacted me on social media were those destitute dropouts I had stopped hanging out with over three months ago. No one from school ever texted me. I didn't even have a social media presence.

Even so, I crossed the room to pick the cell up. Twenty five percent charged and still no messages. Well, if Sarah had wanted to meet me, maybe I'd just got the timing wrong, and she'd contact me again tomorrow. At least I hoped so. I thought of my mother's room down the hall and wondered if Sarah had a warm place to curl up tonight. Then I told myself that someone who had run away as many times as she had would be well practiced in the art of finding a place to sleep.

Laughter made its way up the stairs, which was an unexpected sound since I fully expected Callum to be gone. I dropped my phone back on the bureau and went to open the door a crack. Dishes clattered together in the kitchen and I could make out rush of water streaming from the tap. More muttering. When a cupboard door clattered closed and the silverware drawer rattled, I knew Gramp was making cocoa. His go to activity when he wanted to calm himself. Callum's voice. Then Gramp's.

This could be a long night.

I imagined the two of them getting cozy over a cup and felt both jealous and irritated. I sighed, too exhausted to wait this out. I tapped my fingers against my thigh then went to check my phone again. Still nothing. What were they doing downstairs anyway? Some mutterings about Callum deciding not to go to university, but to stay in town.

I clutched my phone and eased myself off the bed to tiptoe over to the door again. I opened it further so I could hear better.

"Training for my certification now," Callum said.

It was encouraging to hear that Gramp treated Callum as though he was human, that he seemed to know the guy, although up to this point I had never even known he existed. I told myself there was probably plenty of people in town that my grandfather knew that I didn't. Somehow just listening to the two of them made me feel more at ease after the events of the night. Except how did I explain the way my skin felt when he touched me--all electric and unnerving?

It was enough to make my calf itch. I rubbed the top of my foot over it absently, trying to find relief as the conversation continued downstairs. There was a moment when I imagined that if I looked at the skin, I would find a mark there. I even knew exactly what it would look like. Burned in. Like a brand except black as soot. It had been nothing but a hallucination, I told myself. My skin was itching only because I was stressing. I was not going to give in to the thought that it had been true for one second by even lifting my jeans.

"I always thought you'd end up as a doctor or something," Gramp said to him. "Go to school on that wrestling scholarship."

"There was no scholarship, and it wasn't wrestling, it was martial arts," Callum said, not unkindly. "I don't think they give away education for anything except football. Not that it mattered. School wasn't for me. I prefer hard work with my hands. Volunteering at the station is what I love. Changed me."

"Good to hear," Gramp said and I got the feeling there was more behind his comment than a small bit of kindness for a neighbourhood boy. "Your parents would be proud."

Callum chuckled then, and it was a throaty sound that

made me think that if I hadn't been all prickly with him, I might have had a chance to elicit that sound from him. Just hearing it gave me a terrible desire to go down the stairs and see what he might look like without a scowl on his face. I wanted to see if the laughter reached his eyes.

I looked at my cell phone. Still nothing. It had enough charge to last for 20 minutes, but if I went downstairs and plugged it in...

That was when I realized I wanted to go down. Neither of them seemed in a hurry to wrap it up, anyway, and waiting for the phone to charge enough to prove I had received texts at all was an endeavor that made my chest hurt. I just didn't want to be alone right then. I wanted to be drinking a cup of cocoa and laughing along with whatever joke they thought was funny.

So it seemed I had made up my mind. I reached for my charger and the cord trailed along behind me as I ran down the stairs. I could see through the window in the counter that the two of them were sitting across from each other at the table. Steaming mugs of cocoa in front of them. A third mug sat in front of an empty chair.

I couldn't help smiling. He knew me well, I had to give him that. I was about to say something, slip into the room and introduce myself into the conversation when Callum asked my grandfather how he was feeling.

I paused at that and watched as Gramp shrugged with a sense of resignation. "Good enough, I suppose."

"You haven't told her?"

"She's always been a handful," Gramp said. "I didn't

know how she would react. I had hoped to tell her this week."

"And now this mess," Callum guessed.

My grandfather shot him a fleeting smile before lifting his mug to his mouth and swallowing enough to make his throat work. I watched the Adam's apple plunge down his throat and lift again. I couldn't help wondering what it was he was keeping from me that would have him so contemplative as he stared across the table.

I considered showing myself, but the way they sat together, comfortable and intimate, I wanted to see if Gramp would say more. I tried to press myself closer against the wall while still leaving enough open space that I could hear.

"I remember her when she first came," Callum said. "I actually tried to talk to her once."

He was lying. Couldn't Gramp see that? I think I would have noticed him if he'd been anywhere near enough for me to see let alone talk to. A face like that, shoulders like that, didn't blend into the scenery. Something fluttered in my neck. I only realized my hand had gone to my throat when I felt my pulse beneath my fingertips.

"I imagine she raised her hackles like a cornered cat," Gramp said, and while I expected Callum to chuckle at the joke, all he said was that I had been more like a badger.

"Well," Gramp said. "Thanks for giving it the old college try. I imagine most of you didn't notice her at all, so it was a nice gesture."

Callum lifted his mug to his lips and blew on the

surface. "Everyone remembers the troubled new kid. She was quite a celebrity even for those of us in high school. Plus, she didn't exactly blend in."

My throat hurt, listening to that.

"I almost expected her to remember me when she saw me tonight," Callum said. "But she didn't. I guess she made more of an impression on me in those days than I did on her."

Gramp gave a short chuckle. "Wouldn't have mattered if you were right in front of her face. I doubt she would remember anybody. She didn't have any friends. Didn't want any."

It was strange he didn't understand the truth of it when he had understood so much of the rest. I always assumed he'd understood that it was tough for me. It was a small town. They all knew each other. They all knew how long they'd all taken to be potty trained. None of them knew what it was like to be abandoned or to be stuck in foster care or to have to wonder what kind of home you were going to go into or back to. I imagined Sarah, and thought of what she must have had to do over the years to survive.

Gramp shook his head and let go a weary sigh. "I wish I could've been enough for her, but what do you do with a kid like that?"

Any other man and I would've taken that comment as an insult, but coming from the man who had held my hair back while I vomited into his garden and then slept with me on the grass wrapped in two sleeping blankets when I refused to go back into the house, I couldn't take it as anything but what it was. A sense of helplessness.

A twinge of guilt rode down my spine.

I watched as Callum reached across the table and lifted Gramp's mug from in front of him. I thought he would squeeze his hand, and for a second I couldn't bear to look at the two of them. I backed away silently, made my way back up the stairs. So Callum had known me before tonight, had he? He'd known I was "troubled". Now it made sense why he was so insistent on watching me, making me feel as though he thought I had started the fire. It was disappointing, but I shouldn't have been surprised. Even in a town the size of Dyre, things had a way of getting around.

I made my way back up the stairs, trying to avoid the step in the middle that always creaked. That was when my phone vibrated in my hand. I took a peek down at it.

It was shooting off small flickers of blue light. I swiped across the screen so that it would pick up my fingerprint and open without a password.

I heard my own sharp intake of breath when I saw three messages sitting there. I knew my fingers were trembling as they swiped the app open. My breath froze tight in my chest as I read the first one.

It was from Sarah.

OMG. What in the hell happened to the church?

My calf itched. With an absent hand I dug at it through my jeans as I tasted again the oily stink of the confessional, imagined the smell of banana as it squashed in my fingers.

I squeezed my eyes closed. It didn't happen. None of that had happened.

I texted back. I asked where she was.

In the crypt. Are you coming?

Of course I was. A gal didn't just leave her bestie hanging, even if the Angel of Death himself was waiting for her.

CHAPTER 7

I shot off a text asking her if she was still there but got nothing in return. I waited with my cell phone clenched in anxious fingers for the next ten minutes, hoping she would reply. I thought of the nights we had spent in the halfway house, she teaching me by hard knocks what it meant to hold your own against a bully. She rapped me several times on the chin before I finally landed a punch. It had been hard enough that the pain of contact sent a jolt of agony up to my elbow, but she just staggered backward and egged me on. She let me hammer at her as I practiced until she was satisfied I could face a bully.

Now she needed my help. I couldn't just leave her there. It didn't matter how many firemen might be still lurking about the building, how many police might be watching from cars to see if the arsonist returned, I had to risk it. I checked the time on my cell phone. 3:00 AM. Maybe if I was lucky they'd all assumed Callum had taken the arsonist home. Maybe my guilt was a nothing but wary suspicion and they weren't watching the place at all.

I kept telling myself that as I picked my way down the hallway toward the back stairs. The door was dusty and slatted with narrow boards of wood. It had one of those old-fashioned latches that you slid across into a notch. I flicked it open and pulled it, creaking, open. I was fumbling for the light switch when I heard Callum saying his goodbyes out in the hallway.

I took a deep breath, bracing myself. With a light flooding down the narrow stairs, I managed to get a bead on how many of them there were. If I crept down quietly enough, Gramp wouldn't even hear me from the kitchen and I could slip out the back porch and be on my scooter before he realized I was gone. No doubt he would tap on my bedroom door and assume from my silence that I was sleeping or still too angry to talk. He never came in my room uninvited. I doubted tonight would be the night he would start.

I felt a little guilty, but I knew I was doing the right thing.

I made a run for my scooter in the dark and put it in neutral so I could roll it down the driveway and up the street far enough he wouldn't hear me start it up. It choked to life with all the respect of a toddler running through a graveyard.

I slipped into gear and trolled my way back to the church and when I found myself in front of it, it looked even deadlier quiet than it had before the fire. Everything smelled of scorched wood and wet ashes. I blew a long gust of air from tight lips. I looked both ways up and down the street, sideways from property to property to see if there was anyone lurking about, waiting for me to show up again. It seemed the street was empty except for the lone volunteer fireman sitting in his car with his head against his window. With the light from the street lamps, I could see his jaw was slack and his mouth was open. Sleeping.

It wasn't until I was creeping around the back I understood why the firemen hadn't found Sarah in the first place. The door to the crypt wasn't even attached to the church. It stood with its own entry like a mausoleum separate from the main building. A quick pan of the property, with its rolling grounds hinted at a tunnel beneath the earth. If the crypts took up the entire foundation, then finding her could take a while.

I did a quick check of the time on my cell phone. 3:20 AM. The sun would be up in a couple of hours. By then it would be much harder to slip out of the building unnoticed. I'd have to hurry. I gave a thought to whether that would be preferable or not. Maybe I did want them to see me exiting with someone else. Prove I hadn't gone in there and set that damn fire on my own.

However, they might just assume I had an accomplice. Make a few mistakes, and people always assume the worst.

I swallowed down whatever fears still lurked in my subconscious and I forged ahead for the crypt door. I shone my cell phone light on it, using up precious seconds of battery power, but enough to see that the lock had been knocked free at some point. So Sarah had come in this way, no doubt. I pulled the door open and stepped inside. The stairs, as expected, went down for at least half a dozen stone treads before they disappeared into the dark. I couldn't imagine why Sarah would choose to squat in a crypt no matter who she was running from, but I supposed she figured no one would look for her there. Even so. Damned creepy choice. She hitched up a notch in my level of respect for her. She had some guts, that was for sure.

I think I would've taken my chances with a dark alleyway before this God-awful place. I was even beginning to doubt I was right until I realized the cobwebs had been disturbed and hung like bits of lace from the ceiling, their tatters waving in the disturbed air. I counted the steps. Six before darkness would swallow me up.

Too many for comfort.

"Sarah," I shouted down in a hoarse whisper. "Are you down there?"

I cocked my head to listen, closing my eyes to shut off all other sensory information. Nothing came back. Inwardly, I groaned. I'd been hoping she would make this easy for me by not having me trudge down into the dark well of blackness. I scuffed down the six steps and discovered that as I moved, my eyes adjusted to the dark pretty quickly. I ran my hands along the walls to guide me and was relieved to discover they were just made of damp cold stone. The grout in between the rocks had gathered some moss, but that was all. No sticky residue of human blood or any other vile thing.

I was beginning to feel more relaxed the deeper I went until the last step revealed another slatted door at the base.

I shone my cell phone on it. Old wood, very old, pitted with wormholes and dents that looked like someone might have tried to beat their way inside at some point. Someone had joined the slats together by a large hoop of beaten iron and tacked it to the wood with two cross bars. My boot rolled across something hard and I shone the cell phone down at the floor. Several rusted nails had fallen free of the door. Two of them sat next to a discarded Taco Bell wrapper. I smiled, wondering what the spirits of the priests might think to be so defiled by fast food garbage.

At least the door was half ajar. Even if the darkness beyond seemed to be deeper, the wrapper indicated Sarah had come this way. I ran my hand along the door, trying to see if there was some lock embedded in it that would close behind me if I went inside. Nothing. Good.

I craned my head around the door frame.

"Sarah," I whispered again, afraid to disturb the stillness but really wanting to get this over with. No answer. I sighed.

The last thing I wanted to do was run headlong into that space for nothing. Bracing myself with a long deep breath, I pressed the on button on my cell phone again and shone it past the door. Just one more long hallway, but this one filled with pottery urns and shelving. Not so bad. Probably just storage. Maybe those long-deceased monks had left a stash of wine or spirits forgotten in those pottery urns. A bolt of booze right then sounded like the ticket. Bolster my spirits.

I almost stepped past the threshold but thought better of it. As worried as I might be about Sarah, I wasn't stupid. Nor was I all that eager to feel my way through the dark for nothing. Better to check and make sure.

I tapped out a message, checking to see if she was in there at all. If she was, how far in did she think she was? Give me a time, I wrote. Had she walked for ten minutes? Twenty? I waited with the vain hope she would text me back with something in like five minutes or less.

Nothing.

I tapped out another: I'm here, but I can't wait forever. Get back to me if you have your phone on.

Nothing. Surely she'd see the light blinking on her cell phone even if she didn't hear the sound of it hitting her inbox. I stared down at the face of mine, willing it to respond. And as I did so, it occurred to me that she had probably turned off her cell phone to save battery power. She probably only turned it on intermittently to send out a text. Maybe her cell phone had died.

I groaned.

I'd come all this way, and yet it seemed it wasn't fair enough.

I yanked at the door and propped it open with a wayward stone at the base of the steps that had fallen away from the wall. Whatever light from the outside made its way down into the stairwell, could at least shine through and show me a way out if I needed it, kind of like an exit sign. After my experience in the cathedral, real or not, I was as jumpy as an eel in a frying pan. I wished I had brought some string with me. Shades of the Minotaur and Theseus. I laughed at that and that gave me a little bit of courage. There was nothing here but long departed monks and nuns. I doubted any priests had been buried here in the last century. There was nothing to be afraid of. Absolutely nothing.

"Except perhaps psychopaths," I mumbled and the sound of my voice echoed off the walls and bounced back at me.

"I can do this," I said. Not only that, if I kept talking, no doubt Sarah would hear me at some point and that would make things easier. Small bursts of my cell phone to orient myself would help. I noticed several, regular nooks with empty torch sconces and some, older crevices with ancient nubs of wax.

I was several feet in before I realized that the crypt seemed patterned with the same layout as the cathedral above it. By my estimation, I would be coming in through the priest's door, and the narthex would be to my left with the altar to my right. I turned a corner and was relieved to see a series of flickering lights.

Candles. Sarah.

At last.

"There you are," I said. I felt my shoulders sag with relief. I strained into the darkness to make out the form that was sitting cross legged next to half a dozen candles with wicks flickering in the shadows. Her hair wasn't long anymore and tied in a braid, but I would know that heart-shaped face anywhere.

"Hell of a night," I said. "You wouldn't believe what has been going on."

"I think I would," said a voice, but it didn't come from ahead of me, and it certainly wasn't Sarah. I had about two seconds of panic slam through me as I recalled a similar experience from just hours before, and I spun on my heels, fist raised. The cell phone dropped from my hands to the dusty floor. I was all piss and vinegar, ready to take on whatever thing came at me.

Then I realized I recognized the voice. Callum. A flashlight blinked on and panned over me, then passed over me, illuminating the walls of the space. I tried to ignore the leering faces of white skulls staring out at me from dug out crevices just beyond where I stood. I sagged and let my arms fall, half relieved, half irritated.

"What are you doing here?" I demanded of him as I stooped to retrieve my phone. "I told you I didn't set the fire," I said, defensively, and I spun back around, leading his gaze with my arm toward where the candles still flickered. "There's your proof right there."

Sarah sat there, not moving. When I shone my cell phone on her, she didn't even blink. I found myself trying to remember if she slept with her eyes open. I know I tried to plenty enough times back in the day.

"Sarah?" I said. "Tell this idiot I'm here because you texted me. Tell him you asked me to meet you here. Both times now."

I felt Callum come up beside me. He smelled of soap and chocolate.

"Ayla?" Callum whispered. "There isn't anyone there."

"The candles," I said, my brow furrowed. "You see *them*, right?" I wondered if he was being dense or stubborn.

"I see candles," he said. "But nothing else. Who are you talking to?"

I pointed at Sarah as she leaned forward into the candlelight. Thick blonde bangs fringed dove-wing eyebrows. I leaned forward, trying to see the long silver scar on her collarbone that I knew had come from a botched suicide attempt. Despite her wearing a gypsy style blouse that draped open over a delicate chest, the scar didn't show. Blue veins threaded themselves downward from the column of her throat to strangely large breasts for a petite girl. If I could see those details, surely Callum could see an entire girl sitting right in front of him.

"Come on," I demanded of Callum, suddenly aware of a wash of heat flooding my skin. My pulse roared in my ears. "You can't seriously tell me you don't see her. My friend Sarah. She's been missing since before I came to Dyre. She's the one who texted me. She's the one I was telling you about. "

"And you think she's suddenly popped back into sight? After that long?" His voice wasn't patronizing like I expected it to be; instead, it was soothing. Too soothing. As though he were trying to calm a crazy woman on the edge of a ledge.

"I'm not crazy," I said.

When he took my hand and tangled his fingers in mine, I fought him.

"Let go of me," I said. "I won't let you patronize me. She's right there. I know you see her." I turned to beg Sarah to say something.

It was in that moment that I realized something wasn't right. Maybe I should have understood it when she didn't move, but I really got the point when she lifted off the floor without so much as getting to her feet. She hung suspended there like some magical swami. Even then, I assumed I was seeing things. It was so damn dark and the candlelight had a habit of playing tricks with the shadows. But it was when a strange scraping sound started to move across the space that I realized something was really wrong. Even Callum seemed to sense it. His hand squeezed mine.

"Do you hear that?" I said. The hairs on the back of my neck tingled.

He didn't have a chance to answer before something slammed into my temple. It struck me so hard, I saw stars blinking behind my eyelids. I fell to a crouch from instinct and pain, dragging Callum with me. I hunched there, swaying, trying to wait out the ache in my head. I might have moaned out loud as I sucked in breath. It wasn't until Callum's hands gripped the back of my neck and head, tucking me into the crook of his shoulder, I realized the air was full of flying things. I got whacked again on the back of the head, then smashed in the shoulder. I was getting battered from all sides except the one nestled against Callum.

"Sweet Sam," he said into my hair. "What in the hell is happening?"

I tried to peek out past his biceps, but I couldn't see anything. I had to grip him by the forearm and clamber out from his embrace to see anything.

The skulls. They were flying out of the carved nooks they had been stored in for centuries and launching themselves at me.

"No," I heard myself say. "Seriously. This can't be happening. Not again."

Callum's arm went around my waist as he yanked me to my feet. It seemed that whatever was after me, was completely happy to let him alone.

He gripped me by my elbow when I managed to stand, then with his other fist, deflected yet another skull. The unmistakable sound of bone cracking into pieces split the air.

"What do you mean happening again?" he said.

My calf was on fire. Enough that it staggered me and I dug my fingers into his forearms.

"The church," I gasped out. "Something happened to me."

I was vaguely aware I should be scared, that if I recalled what had happened in the church earlier in the evening, I should be running headlong down the hallway toward the crack of light I had left open as an exit sign. I should have grabbed his hand without explanation and just got myself and him the hell out of there.

But some part of me had begun to tingle. I licked my lips, feeling the electricity as though it was dancing on my skin. A strange sort of giddiness made the hairs on my arms stand up.

"It's on," I heard myself say, and it came to my ears as though I were underwater and the words were both magnified and muffled. I imagined myself as some sort of warrior sensing impending battle and wanting, no needing, to confront it.

At least that's how I felt right up until the time the remaining bones lifted from their crannies and sailed toward the skulls that owned them. One by one, they assembled into walking, chattering, rattling skeletons.

"Holy shit," I said.

I wanted to look at Callum to see if he was seeing what I was, but that was when each of them with one loud voice let out an ear-piercing shriek and then ran clattering toward us.

CHAPTER 8

My first instinct wasn't to throw up my fists and jab at whatever came for me. My instinct was run, but I ended up with no option but to duck and weave. And I did it successfully at first until there was an army of assembled skeletons filling the space all around me. The sheer mass of them became a weight that sucked all the breath from my lungs as they converged on us front and back.

Surrounded just like an ambush and there we were in the middle, jumping out of the way of whatever came at us. At least that's what I was doing and assumed it was so of Callum until I heard the sounds of grunting and bones cracking. I threw myself to the dirt, face first, and crawled over to the wall. It seemed to throw the attackers for a moment and, dazed, they stood still for a few seconds as they tried to blindly retrace my path. I shone my cell phone out into the space, hoping to find Sarah somewhere. I panned it over the walls and ahead of me. One skeleton was still rested in a cranny in the wall, its skull sitting nestled between its bones like the proverbial skull and crossbones sign. I panned left, where the worst of the noise was coming from and was met with the sight of Callum methodically kicking through whatever charged at him.

That was it. Action. I had to do something. The sight of him falling to a crouch in a roundhouse kick that swept three skeletons into a heap next to him gave me hope. Especially when they clattered to pieces beneath his strikes. It gave me enough courage to scramble to my feet and hurl myself at the nearest skeleton.

I had never fought anything but solid flesh before, and most times until Sarah had taught me, I had lost. I had always ended up using my bravado, stemming from the confidence that I could use my fists to protect myself after Sarah left. This time, I gave it what I had. Instead of punching head on and ruining my knuckles, I elbowed my way through, thinking only of getting to the other side, of getting to Sarah so we'd be together in one pack, able to face the horde.

I owed her. I couldn't just leave her here, now I'd found her. Trouble was: I couldn't see her through the horde of skeletons.

"We need to get to Sarah," I said to Callum, telling myself they were just bones after all. They couldn't exactly hurt us. I had to be rational about this. They had no weapons. They had no flesh or muscles. All we needed to do was make a path to the door.

I kept telling myself that until one of them bit down

hard on my bicep. Pain lanced through the muscle and I let out a scream that sent me to my knees. I staggered onto my feet again, trying to get through, striking at what I could and wincing when I landed a blow because the bones were hard and brittle and when they broke, they jabbed into me.

"Back off," I yelled and swiped at a tumble of rib bones that struck me on top of the head. I almost made it two steps forward when a pain ripped through my shoulder. I looked frantically around me, seeing but not seeing as more pain shredded into my calves and thighs. They were biting me. From above and below, the jaws were digging into my skin. I gasped in pain, tried to strike out and felt bones connect with hard jolts to my knuckles and elbows.

I was drowning in bones except for the fiery spots of skin where they bit down on me. I flailed around and latched onto something solid but fleshy. Callum's hand reaching for mine through the crowd. My wrist found his hand and he grabbed for it. I felt myself yanked, and almost lost my footing again. Then he yanked harder and I barreled through several bony warriors all at once, breaking them to pieces. They fell to the dirt floor with a loud clatter. I swung back around, making sure they were indeed beaten.

To my horror, half of them reassembled. The other half clutched at rib bones from their comrades and aimed them at us like lances. They leaned forward in a sprinter's lunge. Back feet dug into the dirt for thrust.

"Holy hell," I said. They planned to rush us, if they had

any minds at all to plan.

I realized we were facing the entirely wrong direction. Sarah was somewhere behind us and the exit was past those armed skeletons. I wondered if Callum knew that. I shot a look up at his face. The candlelight was making a grim line of his jaw and I could see beads of sweat running down his hairline.

"We are most royally screwed," I said and he muttered his agreement.

There was a collective roar of clacking as the bones rushed us. Callum yanked me hard against his chest and I spun around into it, wanting shelter no matter where I got it. We pirouetted together like dancers in perfect rhythm and for a second I thought we'd managed to avoid the rush. The smothering scent of soap and musk and the feel of a flannel shirt gave me the false hope that we were reprieved. Then I felt a hot tingle over my calf, making the muscle twitch and spasm.

I sucked in a breath. No doubt one of those things had stabbed me in the calf. They would go for my stomach next. My face. My eyes. I let go a scream but it got muffled in Callum's shirt or his arms, I wasn't sure. I only knew that in the next instant, as I tensed and prepared for a blow, a whooshing sound echoed through the cavern. My hair lifted on end and sailed around me like a flag. There was the distinct sound of pitter patting like hard rain coming down on packed ground.

But in the middle of an underground tunnel, with the quietness of a crypt long forgotten by its followers, there shouldn't have been any wind at all.

I realized in a flash that I was pressed up close to Callum, my arms around his waist and my face burrowed into his armpit.

"They're... Dead," he murmured from above my hair, and I felt everything in his shoulders relax.

The heartbeat against my cheek still thudded like thunder, but it was a heart. A heart. Thank God. Why ever I thought he was inhuman, I knew the difference now as that steady but staccato rhythm thrummed against my ear. I was glad of something solid and human even if the knowledge that I had burrowed as deep as I could into his embrace made my neck flush with heat.

I peeked up into his face, not daring to believe it was over. He waggled his charcoal eyebrows and jerked his chin in the direction of the skeletons.

It was a foolish thing to say, to call them dead, but that's how they looked. They were still assembled, but they had fallen in postures that looked as though they had been slammed hard in the chest. Their legs were splayed wide and their arms flung up over their heads. The jaws gaped open as the skulls lay on their sides.

"What in hell was that?" I said, stooping to rub at my calf. The pain was gone but something electric still had a hold on me. There was a faint buzzing sound in my ears.

"Protection," someone said. A familiar voice.

I peeled myself from Callum's arms and turned to face Sarah. I was still too dumbfounded to register her meaning, but I was so glad to see her, I rushed forward without thinking. I stopped short just a few feet from her when I realized that just a few minutes earlier, she had been floating cross legged in the air. This particular Sarah had short blunt bangs, and black hair, and it was tied into a braid.

"You look different," I said, wary.

"Four years will do that to you," she said with a smile. "You look the same, though. Still skinny and tiny. Same flyaway red hair."

I checked Callum's face for confirmation. Yes. He saw her. He was looking straight at her, following our conversation. I relaxed just a bit.

I looked back over the room to indicate the pile of bones that had moments ago been moving and clacking things, intent on attacking us. I knew it couldn't be a hallucination because Callum had seen it too.

I pointed to them. "You call those things protection?" I said and crossed my arms over my chest. I'd seen enough oddities over the last eight hours that I wouldn't rule anything out, but neither did I want to believe everything I saw. Some of those things were just too far-fetched to be real.

"Want to tell me what's going on?"

She worried her lip for a moment as she took in Callum standing there with his fists clenched at his sides. The shadows playing across her face made her look drained. The Sarah I remembered had been hard-edged, with a look of hard, worn maturity a 14-year-old shouldn't have had. She looked even older now, these four years later, as though grit had embedded itself in her psyche.

"Who is he?" She jabbed her finger in Callum's direction.

"Protection," he said.

It took a few moments, but eventually she smiled and it transformed her face. She was more the girl I had remembered than a mistrustful and jaded woman.

"This is the girl I told you about," I said to him. "Now do you believe me?"

"I don't know what to believe at this point," he said, stealing a look over his shoulder at the dozens of fallen skeletons. He gave a quick shake of his head as though to clear it.

She waved us closer, deeper into the cavern. "Follow me," she said, waving us closer. "It's not safe here."

"No kidding," Callum muttered and I glanced at him. He pressed his lips into a tight line, but I could see the comments flit across his expression one by one.

"You coming?" Sarah urged when neither one of us moved, and I pulled in a bracing breath. I'd come to find her after all. I wasn't about to leave until I heard what she had to say.

"Both of us?" I asked, checking to be sure, and she shrugged.

"You in?" I asked Callum. "You can leave if you want."

I thought as he looked me over, he might hang back, but wanted a few seconds to formulate an excuse. I wouldn't have blamed him if he hightailed it right straight back out, but when he shot a quick look over his shoulder, it seemed to give him some resolution. He threw his shoulders back and lifted his chin.

"What kind of man would I be if I left two kids alone in a creepy crypt?"

Sarah snorted. "I'll be sure to keep that in mind next time I save your hide."

We ended up following her through another wooden door with slats joined together by iron bars. There was less rust on this one, and it pushed open easily and quietly. We stepped into a larger room that by my estimation would have been just below the altar if we were standing in the church above us.

The room was completely lit. The walls were lined with ancient looking iron sconces spaced about every three feet and someone, undoubtedly Sarah, had stuffed them with candles. Wax dripped down the walls in gobs that resembled stalactites. Ages, perhaps centuries, of wax had accumulated and built up beneath her contributions. White wax on the surface blended with dustier looking gobs until a layer of yellow beeswax at the very bottom. I spun in the room, taking it all in.

She had been here for a while, that was evident. She had placed a sleeping bag with a dozen pillows and throw cushions against the wall. They were all threadbare and faded. I got the feeling she had assembled them from a thrift store, and I imagined the only vintage store in town feeling as though it hit the jackpot when she cleared it of old blankets. It made sense. A runaway probably didn't travel with much that didn't fit on her back.

Next to her bed squatted a plastic cooler with a red top.

It was to that cooler that she went when she crossed the room. The top creaked open and she brought out a bottle of water. With a toss, it sailed across the air at me and I caught it thankfully. I twisted it open and guzzled half the bottle in one go before passing it to Callum. He guzzled the rest down and then stood there with it clenched in his hand as he took in the room.

Ignoring his rigid form, I nudged her sleeping bag with my booted toe.

"You look like you've been here a while," I said.

She nodded at me. "Almost a week and a half."

"And you only contacted me last night?" I felt a little betrayed.

"I didn't want to risk your life," she said so matter of factly, I was immediately suspicious. She was lying. Even the little buzzing in my ear paused to assess it.

I narrowed my eyes to little slits of suspicion. "My life?" I said. "Who would be trying to kill me? Is that what that protection was for? Those... Skeletons?"

She held her hand up as though in surrender. "They wouldn't have hurt you. I had them fully under control."

"What do you mean under control?"

She shrugged. "I mean exactly what I said. I spelled them to keep anyone from entering the crypt."

Callum coughed and I slid my gaze sideways to see him with that full mouth of his pressed into a tight line. He wasn't fooling me. I knew he had coughed up the word crazy into his hand, and so did Sarah by the look of her face. To be honest, I might have thought the same thing if I hadn't just seen what I'd seen.

"So it was you who made them stop?"

"Released them," she said. "Yes. That was me."

Callum threw the water bottle onto the sleeping bag and it bounced off onto the dirt floor.

"You make it sound as though they were under your orders or something. As if you didn't notice, those things, those *bones*, have been dead for centuries."

She nodded and eased herself down onto her sleeping bag. "Exactly." She crossed one ankle over the other with her legs stretched out. "That's the kind of thing I do."

I expected a ton of things in that moment, but I certainly didn't expect Callum to charge her and yank her by the elbow back to her feet. He gave her a shake that would have rattled my own teeth.

"I don't know what game you're playing," he said. "But it'll be morning soon and this place is going to be crawling with inspectors."

True to form, she didn't so much as break a fearful look across her face. She simply pulled away and stood with her hands on her hips.

"You think this is a game?" she said. "You think I think it is? Just goes to show how ignorant you both are. Maybe I shouldn't have involved you." She glared at me, then sent an equally hateful glower Callum's way.

"Sarah," I said, pulling her attention away from the glaring Callum. "What's going on? All of this is just –"

"Crazy?" she said and there was an almost manic

gleam in her eye. Even so, I nodded. I felt pretty much like the same gleam was in my own gaze.

"Crazy," I echoed. "That's the word for it, but for what it's worth, that's not what I was going for."

I thought of my time in the church above just hours earlier and my bare escape from a maniac, who by the next maniac's account, was trying to collect my soul so he could regain his wings. If she was standing in front of me admitting she was able to control long dead bones, then I had the feeling that Azrael and his silver-tipped cane had also been all too real.

I thought about the way my calf burned at the strangest of times, the way it was aching even now and I knew that if I looked at it--saw that there was a mark, I wouldn't be able to deny any longer it had really happened. Because it meant that my life was never going to be the same.

Crazy didn't even begin to contain everything I thought about what was going on. I spread my arms wide, watching her face and admitted what I was really thinking.

"It's overwhelming."

Callum snorted and I gave him a warning look. Whatever was going on, however things were changing for me, I knew one thing for certain. I needed to get her out of there.

"Listen," I said to Sarah. "Why don't you come with me? We'll go home, have a good meal--"

"I can't do that," she said, cutting into my well meaning and carefully controlled voice with a panicked note in her voice. "I can't leave here."

"But--"

"But nothing," she said. "I can't go. For the same reason I didn't dare go to your house." She crossed the space to the bundled up bunch of blankets and pillows. She sat down on the biggest cushion, cross legged, and looked up at me.

"I had to make sure I could trust you," she said.

"Of course you can trust me," I said, rushing her. "I texted you when you left, I texted you tons."

"I know," she said. "I got every one."

Callum watched the exchange with obvious impatience. "What neither one of you are even bothering to dance around is what in the hell were those things out there?"

She blinked and peered up at him. "I told you they were protection." She shrugged. "Wardings. Weapons, if you prefer. They're keeping me safe."

"From what?" he asked before I could.

"My family."

"Your family?"

I sagged against the wall, pulling to mind all those stories she had told me in the dead of night when we shared a room in foster care. I'd fancied at the time that she was making them up, that she was adding some imaginative color to the regular old awfulness of abuse that put so many of us into homes in the first place. Even when she'd run away, I told myself that the place she needed escape from must be truly terrible for her to risk living on the streets instead of returning there, but never once did I actually believe the stories.

"But you are of age now, surely," I said, mentally ticking off the months older than me that she was. She should be her own woman by now. She should be working, have her own apartment.

"In my family, age doesn't matter." She reached into the cooler beside her and pulled out a sandwich wrapped in cellophane. She peeled the plastic away and jammed one corner into her mouth. She cocked her eyebrow at me as she chewed.

"So why text me if you didn't want to leave this place?" I said. "What do you want from me? Food, clothes?" I mentally started ticking down all the things a person could possibly need if she had holed herself up in an underground cavern, and I told myself that whatever she wanted, she needed to be rescued more.

She swallowed and pressed a finger to the corner of her mouth, scooping up some errant mustard.

"I don't know," she said. "I'm just tired of running. Tired of being alone."

It was a peculiar thing to hear her voice break, and I crouched in front of her, putting my hands on her knees. I wanted to fix this for her. The dank this was obviously playing on her mind. Making her paranoid.

"We need to get out of here right now," Callum said, a note of urgency in his voice indicating to me he was still clinging to the belief that things were normal despite everything he had just witnessed in the tunnel. "The inspectors will be here soon and they'll find us trespassing, add to that destruction of sacred property..."

"Ah," she said, interrupting him. "We finally get to the point. This place is sacred, which lends me a bit of extra warding. Like my protection out there." She jerked her chin in the direction of the door. "It's why my parents lost me to foster care, why I ran away when they tried to send me back. It's why they're looking for me now."

I was almost afraid to ask, but I did.

"And what reason is that?" I squeezed my eyes closed, bracing myself for the answer.

She let go a long and heavy sigh. "I'm a necromancer. The first true necromancer in two centuries."

"Necromancer?" Callum said, and his tone told me exactly what he thought of her explanation.

I felt as though my teeth were grinding together. Of course. Because this night couldn't get any stranger.

"Necromancer," I said, with my eyes pinned to Sarah's blue eyed gaze. "You raise the dead."

Sarah touched her finger to her nose. Bingo, the motion said, and there was a sad look of in her eyes.

I thought of the psychopath who had cornered me in the church. Covered in tattoos from top to bottom, desperate and deadly because he obviously knew what would happen to him if he didn't succeed in collecting me. I remembered the Angel of Death who had come after that maniac died and I thought of the things he had told me that I was, that I had become. I recalled every word of the things he wanted me to do. The things he said I had to do if I wanted to collect my wings and go home.

I cared about collecting wings I couldn't remember ever having and going to a place I didn't even remember living in about as much as I cared about the shoes I'd grown out of and tossed in the garbage. I'd almost as much said so to him.

I remembered Azrael's words. I could live out this human life without collecting a single fare but I would return to him at the end of it. I wouldn't reincarnate into another human body. Instead, I would be gathered up as a pile of glittering dust and funnel down into the top of his cane. Limbo. I didn't know what that would mean, but it certainly didn't sound pleasant.

I let go a shuddering sigh as all those thoughts made their way through my mind and I faced Sarah with a sense of resignation.

"Then I suppose that means I'm supposed to kill you," I said.

CHAPTER 9

"Kill me?" she said. "But why? What is that supposed to mean?"

Strangely enough, she didn't look alarmed or surprised at my declaration. Just curious. Maybe a little weary. If I gave her careful study, I might think she looked a little sick and pale, but who wouldn't be, living in creepy place like this for nearly two weeks?

I suppose in the end she knew she had nothing to fear from me, or maybe she was just so desensitized to the thought someone wanted to harm her, she didn't have the energy left to be surprised. No doubt she wasn't afraid of me anyway. She had been the one who taught me to defend myself in the first place. She probably thought she could take me if it came to that. Not that it would. I had made my decision back in the cathedral. I didn't care what that Azrael said, and I didn't care what happened to me. I did have a choice and that choice absolutely did not involve killing someone I loved no matter what it cost me in the end.

I shivered as I thought of seeing the Angel of Death again. I hugged myself tight as I paced. It seemed now that I had heard the word necromancer from her own mouth, the buzzing in my ears had grown louder. I had to put my hands up to my ears to try to block out the sound. I even imagined it was Azrael trying to communicate with me, trying to drive me insane enough to become what that thing in the cathedral had become.

I felt her hands on mine, and opened my eyes to see her staring into them. She was shushing me and only then did I realized I had been whimpering.

"I'm alright," I said, backing away, trying to get some distance from her so I could think. I wrapped my arms around my midriff, nodded at her. "I'm fine."

She tried to reach for me, but I stepped away.

"You can't just drop a bomb like that and not explain it," she said.

"Yeah," Callum said warily. "What *are* you saying?"

I couldn't blame him for being suspicious. I had just declared an intent to kill her for heaven's sake. His brain must be ready to implode with all of the strange things it had been forced to process in a short time. And he didn't even have the benefit of being attacked in the cathedral by a tattooed maniac to initiate him into the craziness.

I scuffed the toe of my boot along the floor in front of me, drawing out my first initial in the dirt. It occurred to me that the first letter of my name was also the first letter of the words Azrael and angel. I scuffed the initial back out again. Then I looked up at her.

"Apparently you're not the only one who's special," I said, discovering the words were harder to say than I had thought.

She blinked at me. I caught Callum from the side of my eye leaning against the wall and crossing one ankle over the other. I noticed his face was carefully deadpan. Like he was trying really hard not to show any emotion and was struggling with keeping the disbelief from his face. I couldn't say I blamed him. I wouldn't want to believe any of this either.

I took a deep breath.

"Grim Reaper," I said, pointing at my chest. "I'm a reaper."

I thought I heard Callum behind me choking on a few choice words that sounded an awful lot like sure, figures, of course she would be.

"Yeah," I said to him. "It would've been easier if I had just burned the church down."

He crossed his arms over his chest and turned just enough that he was looking back toward the exit, avoiding me. Sarah, on the other hand, pushed herself to her feet and strolled over to me as though it was most natural thing in the world to have heard. She slapped me on the shoulder with all the pride of a comrade in arms after a good fight.

"I've heard of those," she said and cocked her head at me, inspecting the line of my body. "I thought you would look different, though."

I pursed my lips. "So did I, actually."

I thought of the way that maniac had looked. It was a bit discomforting to think I could possibly end up like that. I pushed the thought away. According to Azrael, that fallen angel had ended up looking that way because he had murdered hundreds, maybe thousands of people. Not people, I corrected myself. Supernatural entities. As though they had some sort of soul in the first place. I didn't even want to start thinking about that. Because none of it mattered. That was not going to happen to me. I still had this life didn't I? Why should I be worried about another one when I didn't even remember it. Whatever I had been before, it was not what I was now. I was human. I didn't care what he said.

Callum had shoved his hands into his jeans pockets and I could tell they were clenched into fists.

"If it makes you feel any better," I said to him. "I just found out about it myself."

His eyes narrowed to slits as he watched me. I felt strangely naked under that gaze. He said nothing but he kept chewing his bottom lip as though he was working out a way to get his mind and his senses to work together in harmony. It made me so damned uncomfortable I felt the need to explain when usually I would have just thrown my hands up in disgust. When I would have given up on anybody else, I felt the need to try and make him believe what was happening. For some reason, I wanted him to believe me.

"It's what happened to me in the church," I said in a rush. "I was there to help Sarah, but I met some maniac –"

"Stop," he said, holding up his hand. "I don't care what fantasies you kids are spinning, but you will not involve me."

He pushed himself off the wall and started pacing. I noticed he avoided the door where we both knew a pile of bones lay in the way of the exit.

"Really?" I said. "You just saw what happened. You just literally went all MMA on a hundred soldiers made of bone and you're going to pretend nothing strange happened?"

"One hundred and four," Sarah corrected and I cocked a brow at her.

"Well," she said. "Get it right if you're gonna state facts."

Callum whirled on her. He was pinching the bridge of his nose and that black hair of his was stuck up everywhere. I realized he had been running his hands through it while I was talking to Sarah.

"I told you not to involve me," he said. I couldn't say I blamed him. I would want out if it was me, but I still felt disappointed. I had hoped for a little more support.

"Like it or not," Sarah said to him. "You *are* involved, and this is not some fantasy. I wish to God it was."

She fanned herself as though she was hot, but it really looked like she was going to faint. She eased herself down onto her bedding again.

"And we're not kids," I piped up. I wasn't sure why that of all things stung the most but it did.

Sarah gave me a queer look, as though that was the least of our troubles and I just shrugged at her. I stole a look at Callum and noticed his jaw was seesawing back and forth. Chewing it over, I guessed. I wondered how long it would take to digest everything. I ran my hand over my stomach absently. I wasn't sure I was even done processing it all. In fact, I felt rather queasy. Every time I got too close to Sarah, something inside hurt. I found myself wondering if maybe she was safer down here, out of harm's way.

"I know it seems crazy," I murmured and pointed in the direction of the skeletons still lying just feet away from us through an ancient door. "But you saw those things coming at us. You know something isn't right. In your heart, you know it."

"I could resurrect them again," Sarah said helpfully and I ran my fingers across my throat in a cutting motion.

Callum cursed. He jammed his hands deeper into his pockets and looked down at the floor, all the while shaking his head.

"Seems like the boy needs proof," Sarah said. "I can give it if you give me a few minutes..." She started rummaging through the cooler.

"Not helping," I said when I noticed Callum trying to freeze her with a look.

Sarah popped up with a plastic bag of something red and soft looking. If I didn't know better, I would have thought it was a hunk of liver. She carefully stored it back in the cooler when she caught me looking at it. She closed the lid with purpose and sat on it, looking over at me with all the seeming innocence of a child.

"Neither of you are helping," Callum hissed.

I sucked my teeth. "Gee," I said. "For a big burly fireman, you certainly are prissy."

He stomped over, stopping a few inches from my face. That smell of soap washed over me, partnered with whatever aftershave he used and for a second everything felt normal. But then he positioned himself just so and the candles along the wall next to him lit his face up perfectly. I could see his expression clearly. It was just one muscle twitch away from collapsing into fury.

"Easy," I said, holding my hands up and waggling my fingers. "I didn't mean anything by it. It's just all really, really –"

"Insane?" he growled. "Because that's what this is. Insanity."

Seven stages of grief, I thought, or its equivalent. Six stages of existential crisis, maybe. I thought for a moment that if he had had to endure what I'd had to suffer alone above us in the cathedral, his journey to belief would've been a hell of a lot shorter. He didn't even believe his own eyes, for Pete's sake. Then, who was I to talk. I'd been denying the ache in my calf since the night I knew I'd been branded, and I realized it was time. I had to face the truth, the same as he did. I yanked my pant leg up to my knee, exposing my calf.

"Look at this," I said, twisting my ankle so I could see the mark that glared up me. I felt queasy looking at it, and seeing exactly how wood-burned it looked. I couldn't stop gawking at it as though any second it would disappear.

It didn't.

I peered up at him. "Does this look like a normal tattoo to you?"

His gaze flicked away but Sarah got up off the cooler and leaned in close. She had to push him aside to get a close look, but when she did she whistled and reached out with tentative fingers to trace the edges. I flinched as her touch met my skin and an electric jolt made its way up my spine. Some place between my shoulder blades burned. She smelled of must and smoke as though she had been down here for years not weeks. I wondered if that was the smell of a necromancer. The smell of death.

"Virtue," she said pensively and peered up at me.

Her complexion was as yellow as the beeswax but her grin made her seem hale. Just the lighting I guessed.

"That's what it says, I think."

"It actually says something?" I wasn't sure why that made me feel itchy all over.

I tried not to concentrate on the way my skin felt like it was trying to tear apart at the base of my ribcage. I held my breath until she retracted her fingers and they hovered over the tattoo instead as she looked up at me. Her bottom lip pressed up into her top in a thoughtful way. Modest but proud at the same time.

"I've had to read a lot of runes. Some sort of natural ability, I guess. That one's pretty ancient."

"Ancient as in?"

"Ancient as in before even Mesopotamia. Although I think they were the first to record it." She put her finger to her lip in thought as she crouched there on her haunches. "Maybe even angelic," she said.

"Stop," Callum said, scuffing toward the door. "Just stop."

I glared at him. "Do you have any idea what happened to me tonight?" I asked. "I went into that dark church to help a friend and I ended up fighting for my life against some maniac. But of course you wouldn't know that because when I killed him, he dissolved in to a pile of ashes that swirled into some glittery dust and disappeared into the top of the Angel of Death's cane." I planted my feet apart, bracing myself. I was breathless with desperation.

"How's that for crazy?"

I watched as his Adam's apple plunged down into his throat. He had his hand on the latch, but he didn't yank the door open.

"Maybe you can forget all this happened," I said, twisting my calf toward him so that he could take in the full tattoo. "I hope for your sake you can, but I don't think either Sara or I will have that luxury."

"Damn straight," Sarah piped up. "Testify, sister."

"All right," he said with a beleaguered sigh. "True or not, let's just get the hell out of here."

He looked around with distaste, one last look of a room he never wanted to see again as his fist pulled at the latch. The door stuck for a second, but then it let go with a burp. He cocked his brow at us, impatient and authoritarian. I almost pitied him.

"I'm going to go down the hallway," he said. "Make sure everything is safe."

"It will be," Sarah said with a sigh. "They're my protection, remember?"

He was shaking his head as he yanked the door wide and plunged into the darkness. For a moment, I wanted to call him back. So many things had been going wrong tonight, I didn't want him to be alone out there.

"Right," I said and headed for the cooler, thinking to pick it up and cart it with us. "We can go back to my place. You can stay the night there and we'll figure out the rest of it in the morning."

Sarah sighed heavily and leaned backward so that her shoulders were against the cold stone wall.

"I told you," she said. "I can't leave. Not yet. It's too dangerous."

"Not if you come to my house," I said. "No one will know you're there."

"You don't get it," she said. "This place is sacred. As long as I'm here in Dyre," she said. "This is the safest place for me. With all of this divinity around, all of these blessed souls, my family's magic can't track me."

"You didn't mention your family were necromancers," I said carefully.

She gave a sort of half smile that seemed both pleased and resigned. "They're sorcerers, actually. Some sort of old family prophecy about the chosen one bringing back the strongest necromancer ever. Rumored to be able to give us true immortality."

"Let me guess," I said, thinking that with the way everything had been going the last few hours, I knew exactly who that was. "You're the chosen one."

"Bitch, isn't it?" she said.

"But you can't stay here," I said. "Not forever."

"I'll stay as long as I have to," she said and I saw in that moment how tired she was. It was etched over every muscle of her face and the sag of her shoulders. "I don't have any choice."

"Everyone has a choice," I said.

"It's not that easy," she said, shaking her head. "They'll come for me. And they'll do anything to retrieve me. I can't risk you or your grandfather or that handsome but glowering hero out there."

"So I'll just take them out," I said. "After all, I'm some sort of bad ass Grim Reaper now."

She cocked her head at me. "Who apparently is supposed to kill me," she said with a grin tugging at her mouth.

I blinked stupidly. I had forgotten that. I squirmed as I remembered the glittering dust funneling into Azrael's cane. I shook my head without realizing I was doing it.

She laid her hand on my arm, comforting. "I'm just messing with you, Ayla. Grim Reapers have no dominion over supernatural beings. You couldn't reap me if you tried." She pursed her lips thoughtfully. "You might be able to kill me," she said, thoughtful. "But you couldn't reap me."

"Because you have no souls?" I guessed and I felt an incredible relief wash over me. Maybe I had got it all wrong. Maybe I had misunderstood because I was so scared.

"Well we do have a sort of essence," she said in an absent-minded way. "There are creatures who do collect our essences, but you'd have to --"

I gathered by the way she halted midsentence she could see the look of horror I felt creeping over my face.

"Don't tell me," she said. "You're Nathelium."

I nodded slowly, almost afraid of her reaction.

"You can't be," she said. "You're fallen?"

Another nod because I couldn't trust my voice.

"You're a fallen one who collects the essences of those who are not mortal?"

"Apparently so," I said trying to put in how sorry I felt to share that awful truth. I watched her expression shift from disbelief to realization and then to fear.

"I'm not doing it," I said. "I don't care what the angel of death says will happen, I don't care about some life eons ago that I don't remember." I almost told her that I didn't care what would happen to me if I didn't collect her up, but I stopped short because I truly couldn't see me doing it. It was inhuman thing to do, to kill someone, and I was human. For this incarnation, my last incarnation, I would be human.

"Angel of death, huh?" she said with a narrowed gaze. "Honey, you have to fill me in."

I shrugged. "There's not much to tell," I said and she

cocked a blonde brow.

"When we're home," I said. "And fed. And slept the sleep of the dead."

She tapped her fingernails along her teeth. "A shower does sound divine. And a hot meal." There was a longing in her voice that made me want to encourage her, but she paused just as I opened my mouth to seal the deal.

"But I can't," she said and blew out a long, resigned sigh. "I don't dare."

I eyed the cooler. "Your supplies must be running low."

She blinked at me.

"And you looked awful tired."

She was giving in. I knew it. I knew I'd won.

She tugged at her braid, pulling it forward and sticking the tip of it in her mouth. She chewed on it for a moment reflectively, her brow furrowed. Bits of black hair poked out the other corner.

I stooped to start picking up the throw pillows and tucked one under my arm.

"You dyed your hair," I said.

"Fat lot of good it did me," she said. She lifted the tip of the braid inspected the ends. "I miss the blonde."

She crossed her arms over her chest, hugging herself. I had the feeling it was taking more than a little courage for her to decide to leave. Her gaze swung from the sleeping bag along the floor with its threadbare throw pillows and cell phone. With a great, shuddering inhale, she shook her hands out.

"Okay," she said. "I'm good." She tugged at her braid

and threw the pony tail back over her shoulder. For the first time, I could see the roots of her blonde hair as she stooped to pick up her cell phone and shoved it into her pocket.

We were already to the door, carrying a candle in each hand for light when Callum appeared close to the outer exit. He had cleared a path through the skeletons, even placing a few of the skulls back into their crannies in the wall. He looked a little less shocked. As if the very act of it had solidified the entire situation for him. I sent him a thready smile that he returned.

It took me a moment to realize something hovered in the air behind him. Something that looked an awful lot like Sarah. Cross legged and blonde haired, this thing wavered in and out, getting steadily more solid as I watched.

"You're still behind me, right?" I said over my shoulder. "That thing isn't really you, is it?"

A quiet word from behind me. "No."

I felt every muscle in my body begin to burn. "Then what the hell is it?" I said, but had a feeling I already knew that whatever it was, it was something that carried even more of a wallop for a supernatural reaper than the human necromancer standing behind me.

"That," Sarah said from behind me, "is my doppelgänger And it doesn't look happy."

CHAPTER 10

There were a few things I never thought I would see in my lifetime, and even less that I thought I would do. A true harbinger of death was not in my realm of possible stops along my lifetime sightseeing tour, but screaming in terror because one has suddenly popped up out of nowhere certainly wasn't out of the question. I think Sarah must have realized I was about to let loose with a shriek that would pierce the otherworld and figured with all her experience, it was probably not the right thing to do at the moment. Not with Callum standing there, totally oblivious to the thing hovering behind him.

I felt her hand slip into mine and squeeze. One small almost imperceptible whisper moved along my hair.

"Don't move," she said.

No problem. My feet were stuck to the earth as though I'd suddenly grown roots. I had no idea what a harbinger could do, but if it scared Sarah, it certainly bore the offering of a little careful respect.

I peered over my shoulder at her, thinking she would at least know what the next step was.

"Something isn't right." She stood as rooted to the floor of the tunnel as I was, her hands working in the air as though she was searching for something. I realized in an instant that whatever she had left back in the cooler was critical for whatever it was that she did to weave whatever spells a necromancer threaded together.

"Can it hurt us?" I rasped out. I was thinking mostly of Callum right in front of it. I kept my eye on the thing behind him, too afraid to let on something was there and wanting desperately to yell at him to get out of the way.

I heard Sarah shuffling around behind me, almost as though she was trying to use me as a shield.

"Can you do something?" I said.

"Not without my stuff," She hesitated over the word stuff as though she was going to say something else and I swallowed down my distaste. It might not have been liver I'd seen in that bag, but it was something equally distasteful. Raw innards of something or other.

"It can't touch us, right?" I said. "It's just a ghostly type thing."

She sighed. "Normally, But this one has been empowered with the ability to kill or incapacitate."

Her hand reached out for mine in the dark as the other one gently placed her candle into an cranny next to a skull. The light flickered as it moved.

"It won't kill me," she said and I realized with horror

she'd stressed the personal pronoun.

"Great," I muttered. The thing behind Callum was most definitely almost solid. In seconds, it would be right there and he would either realize it stood behind him or it would do something awful like snap his neck before he could draw another breath.

I decided to take a chance. After all, I had taken down a fully-fledged supernatural reaper with nothing but a shard of glass.

I was already charging ahead, shrieking like a banshee, when the thing fully solidified behind Callum. The look on his face might been comical as he caught sight of me hurtling at him through the gloom of the tunnel, except the thing behind him wrapped its arms around his waist and lifted him clean off the floor. I ran straight through where he had once stood and slammed into the door.

I fell backward onto my ass and bit down hard on my tongue as I landed. One of my elbows rammed into something solid, a rock or a bone. Out of instinct, I rolled over onto my side and cradled the aching and buzzing joint, moaning out loud through a mouth that tasted of blood.

Too late, I realized I had left my back to the doppelgänger above me and Callum's wildly thrashing feet. One of his boots connected with the back of my head and I fell flat.

The pain didn't hit for at least two seconds, but when it did, it pulled a whimper from me. I wasn't ready for this. I had foolishly thought that because I had been lucky with the reaper who had come to collect me, that I'd somehow imbibed some special skills or power from his death. Hadn't Azrael told me so? Well if it had, it certainly didn't include mad fighting skills. All I could do beneath that horrific thing above me was try to claw my way out from beneath it.

I flipped over onto my back, and tried to crab myself back into the tunnel toward Sarah. In that time, I realized that the reason Callum was thrashing around so desperately was because the thing had shifted its grip to his throat and was choking him with one hand. I tried to claw my way to my feet and went momentarily blind as another blast of pain struck. That was when I realized the thing's gnarled fingers had tangled into my hair and was pulling me off the floor to a staggering stand.

I could feel clumps of hair tearing from my scalp, sending a line of fire streaking across the top of my head. I panted in pain and strained for the floor with the tips of my toes to ease off some of the pressure. I called up long nights of training and punched out at the thing, hoping to connect with something solid.

Instead, even as my quick jabs snapped out, the doppelgänger's reach magically extended as it shifted its shape and transformed into something that resembled a troll from a child's fairy tale.

I had good, clear vision of the thing, with its long jowls that dripped foaming orange saliva onto the floor of the tunnel. I could swear I heard its spit sizzle as it struck the hard packed earth beneath me. The thing's teeth reminded me of a shark's double row of incisors, and as its gaze landed on me, I thought I could make out in the depths of its yellow eyes the flash of recognition. It howled in laughter and shook me, lifting me higher from the floor. I heard Callum gagging as he fought. I could feel each thrust he made as he twisted in the thing's grip.

We dangled there together, and I watched helplessly as Callum's green eyes popped wide open as his thick fingers worked at the hand around his throat. He was struggling fiercely, kicking at whatever he could connect with and twice his boots knocked into my shins, eliciting shrieks of pain from me that made the creature chuckle all the more. My hands went to my hair automatically and then recoiled as I felt the slimy knuckles of the doppelgänger.

I didn't know what to do. Terror was all my mind could register. I felt soaked in adrenaline as every muscle in my body twitched to free itself even as my mind blanked out. I reached out for Callum, thinking that in our last moments, he would want to feel something human. Something warm and flesh covered. I knew I wanted it, that last bit of human touch before Azrael came to collect me up in a glittering pile of ash into the top of his cane.

Hot tears streamed down my face as I thought about that very strong possibility and as I tried to search through watery eyes for Callum's face, my fingers found his waist. With every ounce of my body screaming to work at being released, I fought to hold on to him. If I could just prop him up with my weight, maybe he could work his way free.

Somewhere through the haze of panic, I heard

chanting. But there was also the sound of rattling bones again, and I knew exactly what that sound meant. The army had been resurrected and they were on the march. I just hoped they knew who the enemy was. I expected them to rush forward with bits of bone and ribs again, but instead I heard the dull thud of something hitting the ground. Stones. Rocks. All sizes and shapes were missiling their way through the air around me.

Dirt sprayed around me, peppering my face and hair. Some of it struck the corner of my mouth and flew inside, leaving me sputtering on the taste of mould and debris.

"Sweet heaven," I said. "They're stoning us." I tried to catch Callum's legs but he was kicking too fiercely.

Something struck me in the chest and made me gasp. I wasn't sure of the size of the rock that hit me, but it felt big enough to have done damage. My rib cage would be bruised for days if I manage to get out of there. If. It was a pretty big order at that point. As long as I was being held by the harbinger I'd be a target. If I didn't live through this, I'd end up as so much glitter in the top of an elderly man's cane.

Right. Not going to happen.

"We need to get free," I shouted at Callum. "Give me your legs. Trust me."

He stopped kicking and for a second I thought maybe he had gone unconscious, but I could still hear the gurgling in his throat. Alive, then. Still conscious. That was a good sign. I sucked in a breath, telling myself it would only hurt for a minute. Surely a few seconds of pain was worth a lifetime.

I braced myself with my palms against the revolting creature's chest and pulled. The burning pain in my scalp let go. I fell, face first, to the floor of the tunnel and it was only some quick instinct that made me roll under Callum's feet.

"Stand up," I hollered, and realized even as Callum's full weight came down on my back, I didn't need to help him. He fell on top of me like dead weight and pushed the air from my limbs in one gust. I gagged on the last remnants of air as I choked to suck it back in.

It took several moments of my chest heaving before I managed to feed enough oxygen to my lungs to breathe without wheezing. I rolled over onto my side, facing the other end of the tunnel. Sarah stood there clenching something plump and red that leaked red fluid through her fingers. Her face was covered in blood. Candles burned all around her.

Callum was coughing somewhere to my side. The harbinger touched ground. I could feel its breath on the back of my neck. I had to get up. I had to run.

I had made it to a sprinter's lunge when Sarah shouted a word I supposed would sound the same in any language: attack, and her army of bones lifted from the ground as one unit and with a great shriek hurtled toward us.

Half a dozen of them slammed into me, knocking me on the cheek and temple and taking the wind from me again. I fell backwards one more time, but this time I wasn't lucky enough to fall free of debris. My head struck the rock that I had used to prop open the door and I lay for a long moment unable to move. I prayed I wouldn't black out. I wanted to see what came at me.

I tried to roll onto my side and push myself onto my elbow, but I collapsed again, my muscles spent and weak. The doppelgänger had decided it was me who posed the most threat, even though I couldn't get up.

"Seriously," I said, thinking of Callum and the way he was lying next to me coughing. "He's a hell of a lot stronger than me."

I sought out Sarah and found her struggling to walk forward, a look on her face that would've terrified me if I hadn't just stared into the pageant winner.

"Do something," I said.

She took one look at me and took a shuddering breath before she collapsed to her knees. She reached out with one hand and made a wrenching motion as though she was opening a door. Light flooded the space and washed over me. In that one second, it bathed the tunnel, and everything inside except the sound of ragged breathing either disappeared or fell to a clattering heap.

A look of relief washed over her face and I knew it was over.

"Thank God," I said.

She gave me a weak smile and then fell over in a crumpled heap.

I think I called out her name but it all got lost as I tried to push myself to my feet and run to her. My knees went weak and I collapsed. It was only Callum's strong arms beneath my knees that made me realize I had probably twisted my ankle. Like he had hours before, he started to hoist me against his chest.

"I don't need saving," I said. "Get Sarah."

The black line of his brows knit together but he nodded and scuffled to the back of the tunnel. I watched him hoist her into his arms and carry her out into the daylight. I started to shiver, whether it was the flood of adrenaline or terror or post traumatic stress, I quaked as though I was a leaf in the wind. I squeezed my eyes closed, because I didn't want to see what was around me. I didn't want to remember it. I knew I'd be seeing it all in my nightmares for months to come.

It seemed an incredible amount of time before I heard his boots on the stone steps again and his shadow fell across me as he came to the door. I lifted my face to see him kneeling down for me.

"Sarah," I said.

"Don't worry," he said and his voice was a ghost of itself, with nothing but a harsh rasp to help it carry. "Her vitals are good."

If I had to explain how wonderful his arms felt as they slipped beneath my knees, I would have to use the word heaven. But there was no way I could describe the relief I felt as I was lifted out of that dark and moldy place and was carried up the stairs to the surface.

When the warmth of the sun hit my face, I realized I was crying. I could see where he'd lain Sarah just at the edge of the parking lot where the grass met pave. It was still early morning yet, perhaps just past dawn, but the sun was high enough already I could make out how incredibly pale she looked in the light. I wondered how long it had been since she'd had a decent meal or a decent night's sleep. Judging by the things we had encountered in the crypt, I imagined it had been months.

Callum eased me down onto the grass that bordered the parking lot just half a foot or so away from her and knelt down next to me. The grass was still wet with dew, and the ache of early fall crispness soaked into my clothes, making me shiver. I looked sideways at Sarah and noticed he had lain his jacket over her. I reached out to touch her arm. Warm. I let out a stuttering breath. Thank God. We were okay. We were all okay.

He cupped my jawline with both of his hands, the fingers sneaking in behind my hair and kneading the back of my neck. I pressed backward into the warmth of his hand, not caring that his peculiar tingling feeling had started running its way down my spine. I was just so glad to be out of there. Safe. His warm, calloused thumb whispered over the crest of my cheek where the tears had started to pool.

"You did good," he said, pinning that green eyed gaze to mine. There was a rasp in his voice that hadn't been there before. "You did damn good."

I nodded, not trusting my voice. I had a hard time swallowing past the clump of relief in my throat. I made small hiccuping sounds and had to hold my breath to get it under control. I didn't feel as though I'd done good. I felt like I'd just failed a very big test.

"I'm putting her in my car," he said, peering down at me. I felt lost in his gaze but I managed to waggle my head up and down.

"You stay here until I come back," he said.

I didn't think I could so much as wiggle my foot.

"I won't move." There. That came out just fine. Not terror-laden at all.

"Good," he said. With an an ease I wouldn't have expected from a man who had just nearly choked to death, he lifted Sarah into his arms again and hitched her high against his chest. Her head rolled back against his arm.

"She's breathing," he said, catching my eye and obviously reading the worry in my gaze. "Her heart rate is fine, so I think she's just passed out. But I think we should take her to the hospital."

Again I nodded. I knew if I tried to speak again, I would break down.

He was only gone for a few moments and when he came back, he knelt down in front of me and used his thumbs to tilt my chin upward as his fingers cupped the back of my neck.

"Thank you," he said.

For a moment I thought he wanted to say more, and the way his eyes trailed down to my mouth, I thought perhaps he was waiting for me to say something. I searched for the right words. Something that could say everything and at the same time carry the weight of all we had just been through together.

"I told you I wasn't lying," were the ones my tongue selected.

CHAPTER 11

The drive to the hospital was a blur. I sat on my side of the passenger seat and stared out the window with my hands clenched between my knees. I'm sure I watched the houses go by for the seven or eight blocks it took to get to the hospital, but I don't remember seeing much that was memorable. Except the sunrise. It had reached over the tops of the trees by the time we sped the distance and was painting a flare onto the car window that made me squint. I had visions of feathers falling from the clouds and felt as though everything around me was buzzing. I was pretty sure that if there was such a thing as an aura, mine was jagged and screaming in bile yellow.

Once, I dared to look over my shoulder at Sarah as she lay in the back seat and I noticed Callum had replaced his jacket with an old plaid blanket and had tucked two of her pillows beneath her head and one beneath her knees. When he had time to do that, I wouldn't remember. All I could think about was facing that horrible thing and failing. I had assumed I was special. I had believed I could make a difference. Now Sarah lay there unconscious. She looked incredibly pale and her chest barely rose and fell.

There was a moment when I thought Callum was going to reach for my hand. His fingers trailed over the stick shift and rested on the side of my seat. From the corner of my eye, I could see how sooty his nails were with embedded ash and dirt from the tunnel. Each crease in the knuckles was lined in black. It was the most incredible thing I'd seen the whole night, those narrow black lines. They reminded me I was alive, and I wanted very badly to take his hand and hold it to my chest because I felt an incredible need to feel normal with good old-fashioned human contact.

Something kept me from doing it, though. Instead, I tightened my grip on my hands with my knees. I had to remind myself that something in me didn't feel as though this guy was quite right. Except for the fact that the doppelgänger had been able to nearly kill him, I still wasn't exactly sure he was human. I didn't know who was human anymore. I certainly couldn't count on the evidence of my eyes at any rate. They had failed me when I'd gone into the tunnel and seen Sarah's hair wasn't right but hadn't bothered to question it.

I had to use all of my senses. Now that I knew there really were monsters and bogeymen, I couldn't just rely on the simple things like sight the way everyday folk did. I had to tune my instincts and my perception of things. If I wanted to live and thrive in a world where there were things not of this world, then I had to recognize those things when I saw them. I'd start with Callum.

I said nothing to him as he pulled the car up in front of the hospital and leapt from his side of the car and headed for the hospital doors. I said nothing when he yelled over his shoulder at me that he'd be right back, and then he tore into the front doors. Seconds later, two burly orderlies pushed out the front with a stretcher between them and a tall pole holding onto a clear plastic bag of fluid. He stood next to the paramedics as they eased her out of the car and onto the stretcher. He looked huge next to them, broad-shouldered and glowering as though he wanted to make sure they handled her correctly. For the first time, I noticed how fine his features were for such a large man and I mentally had to remind myself that he was only a few years older than me.

It was only when I saw Sarah starting to struggle that I said anything at all. It looked like they were hurting her.

"Leave her be," I hollered out the window at the paramedic who was holding her down and ramming something into her arm. He ignored me.

I yanked my door open and jumped out of the car. They were already wheeling her off and I could see her fighting to get off the stretcher. She was yelling something about not being safe. Begging them to let her up.

Despite my resolve not to speak to him until I had figured out what he was, my panicked gaze went straight to Callum. "What are they doing to her?"

"She's going to be alright," he said, sweeping that green

eyed gaze over me and making me want to shiver. "She just needs some rest. Real rest. They're giving her a sedative."

A sedative. She'd be helpless. I started to run for the doors behind them. "They can't do that," I said.

I felt his grip on my elbow, holding me back, spinning me around to face him. That jolt of electricity went up my arm again. It made me dizzy and I felt my knees go weak. It was worse when I looked in his eyes. They were so damned penetrating. I thought they could look right straight into the curled up balls of my mind.

"Ayla," he murmured. "They know what they're doing. She's not well. Even you have to admit that."

"But she doesn't feel safe."

"But she is safe." He ran a thumb over the crease in my elbow, making the hairs stand on end. I yanked my arm away.

"How do you know she's safe? Anything could happen to her in there."

He looked hurt I'd pulled away from him, but that was the least of my worries. I pulled my arms across my chest, gripping the backs of my shoulders with my hands. I was having a hard time staying on my feet. Everything was swimming around me.

"Don't worry," he said. "I'll stay here with her. I won't let anything happen to her."

I knew he was patronizing me. Any regular person would have believed a woman was safe in the hospital. But I wasn't a regular woman anymore. Sarah wasn't either. We'd seen things. We'd fought things.

"That thing back there —"

"Is gone," he said. "And I doubt it's going to come back in a hospital filled with people."

He didn't sound convinced, but I think we were both willing to believe it. I swallowed, nodding because I knew he would have to be right. She really should be checked out. I started to fish my cell phone out of my pocket to call my grandfather. The least I could do was make sure there was a place for her to go when they released her.

"Crap," I said as I tried to tap it to life. "Dead."

"Mine too," he said, reaching for my elbow again and this time I let him guide me into the building. He checked with the registration nurse to find where they had taken her. Then we went up the elevator to the floor she was on and sat in two plastic industrial chairs with out of date magazines lying on a table in front of us.

I sat in the waiting room's plastic chairs while Callum made the executive decision to find a pay phone and call my grandfather. I gave a vague thought to how worried he might be that Callum was calling instead of me, but I knew I couldn't make up an excuse for why I had been out all night or why I wasn't coming home for a few more hours. I was happy to let Callum tell him whatever he wanted to hear and deal with the rest of it later.

He returned with a slight smile. Some success, at least. I didn't bother to ask what he told my grandfather, but I could see that he had been running his hands through his hair and there was black stubble on his chin. In the full light of the hospital lamps I could see how dusty his hair was from our encounter in the tunnels. He had a bruise along his throat, and I ran my fingers along the column of my own, wondering what it would have felt like to be gasping for air and be unable to wrest the fingers from your throat that were cutting it off. I swallowed, testing the feel of my throat muscles against the pads of my fingers. It made me feel claustrophobic.

His struggles hadn't been acted out. There was no way you could make that panicked set of movements unless you really couldn't breathe. Self-preservation was a uniquely mortal thing to do, I figured. Would a supernatural creature be worried about dying in such a mortal way? I studied his profile quietly as I contemplated those things.

I decided he must be mortal if not human. The rest of it I could work out later.

He turned to me during a time when I was riveted by the pulse in his throat and a slight smile tugged at the corner of his mouth. While I managed to tug my gaze from the pulse in his throat, it didn't go much further than his mouth. I told myself that I was too stupefied by fatigue to lift my eyes further, but I didn't argue with myself over how soft those lips looked. I couldn't focus on much more than the way they shaped their words when he spoke to me.

"You really need to get some sleep," he said. "Why don't you let me take you home."

I shook my head. I couldn't leave her. I forced her to leave that crypt and now she was in danger.

"I want to be here when she wakes up."

"I checked with the nurse, they said that was going to take a while."

"Then I want to be here until she wakes up."

He sighed and leaned closer. That soapy smell of him washed over me again and I inched away, afraid he might touch me and ruin my resolve to decide upon his mortality.

"Here's what I know," he said. "They said she's suffering from adrenal fatigue. Slightly malnourished. They want to keep her in for a couple of days to make sure she gets the nutrients she needs."

I nodded my head slowly. It sounded like there was something else coming. As if to confirm it, he shifted in his seat, facing me head-on.

"They wanted to know her specifics. Next of kin. Birth date."

I chewed the inside of my cheek, thinking how grateful I was that she had never given me any of that information.

"I couldn't tell them I was related because they know me. They know my whole family. But they don't know you. Well..not well anyway. I said she was your cousin. Visiting from the city."

I waggled my head up and down. That sounded about right. We could get away with that. Then I realized it might not fly for long.

"But Gramp," I said.

"I told him you were with me and that I would bring you home. You're going to have to handle the rest of it." The backs of his fingers whispered along my jawline, and I imagined he must be feeling pretty fatigued too because they lingered there just a little too long in the crook between my earlobe and jaw. I almost enjoyed the tingle until I realized he was staring at me.

"What?" I said.

"You're going to have to explain all of it." He gave me a look indicating he meant to him. He'd obviously seen enough he believed me when I said I'd been searching for Sarah when the cathedral caught fire, but whether or not he would believe the rest of it, I had my doubts. I tapped my finger on my thigh, thinking. I barely believed it all myself.

"I still want to stay here until she's awake."

"She'll be out for at least a couple of hours. And you need some rest too."

I chewed the bottom of my lip. I didn't feel right about any of this. But I *was* exhausted. Every part of me, including the backs of my thighs, wanted to do nothing but fall into a coma for a few hours.

Still, the protest was a habit I couldn't quite give up.

"I can't just go home when she's alone in there."

"And what about your grandfather?" he said. "Doesn't he deserve to know what's going on?"

I cocked a brow at him. "And how would you describe what went on here?"

To his credit, he didn't reply. Instead, he just got to his feet and held out his hand. I looked at it for a long time before I lay my palm against his. I waited, braced, for that feeling of electricity and when it came I squeezed my eyes closed, trying to work out what it might mean. I let it wash over me, tingling across my skin and riding my spine. I decided it didn't hurt, the electricity. I realized that in a way, it felt comforting. Familiar.

I opened my eyes to see him watching me.

"You trust me now?" he said and his gaze fell to my throat where I knew my pulse was racing.

"Maybe not trust," I said. Trust was such a hard thing. "But I believe in you, and that's saying something."

"Then let me take you home."

I let him help me to my feet. His hand left mine long enough to move to the small of my back as he guided me from the waiting room to the elevators. He gave me at least three feet of space inside the cabin as it went down the four floors to the lobby. Then he gave me the fifteen minutes of silence I needed on the way home to collect my thoughts.

I stole a glance at him to check and see if the bruise on his throat was still there. It was darker and bigger and if I looked at it long enough, I could make out the size of the fingers of the thing that had wrapped its hand around it. I thought of him struggling to live beneath the vice-like grip of that thing and I realized as he pulled into my driveway, he probably should have gotten checked out at the hospital as well.

For some reason, it seemed very characteristic he hadn't requested any care for himself.

I put my hand on the knob of the door and I gave him a small, timid smile over my shoulder. It was all I had in me, but I hoped he would understand it meant more than any words I could conjure.

I had every intention of pulling the latch and releasing the door, but for some reason I hesitated. It was only when he reached across the car and laid his hand on mine I realized why. I wanted to feel that touch again. His fingers slipped around my wrist. He was touching my pulse, I thought. His thumb even moved like a caress over the skin and I could feel it press into the spot where my heart beat could be felt.

"Goodnight, Ayla," he said with a different sort of rasp than had been in his voice earlier. Then he let go my hand and gripped the stick shift, looking straight ahead through the window.

I scrambled from the car awash in confusion and a strange excitement that lit my feet as I ran for the door.

CHAPTER 12

In the end, I didn't have to say anything to Gramp. I don't know what Callum told him on the phone, but he didn't question me when I held up my hand as I closed the door behind me. I knew if I opened my mouth to say anything I would break down and cry. I didn't want that to happen, and maybe that's why he didn't question me. He knew me well after all. He just passed me a cup of warm cocoa and lay his hand on the top of my head. I could feel the heat of it, of him, radiating over me. I almost broke down then. With a small, tight smile, he turned away from me and went back into the kitchen to rattle pots and pans. I went up to my room, plunged my charger into my phone and fell onto my bed fully clothed.

When I woke it was dark. The clock on my bedside said 6 PM. I'd slept all day, and probably right through supper. My first thought when I realized where I was and that I was safe, was of Sarah. I had to get to the hospital. I was sure her sedative had wore off by now and by this time of evening they'd be allowing visitors in. I grabbed a quick shower and stampeded down the stairs, phone in hand.

I stopped short on the stairs when I saw Callum sitting in the dining room sitting across the table from my grandfather. Like the night before, there were three places set.

"Funny," I said. "I've never seen you in my house before and now twice in two days this old man is breaking bread with you across his table."

Callum looked up at me with fork poised halfway to his mouth. I recognized Mediterranean pea salad, my favorite, and my stomach growled loud enough to make Callum's eyebrow quirk.

"Your grandfather and I go way back," he said.

"Do you?" I eyed the big bowl of salad in the middle of the table and chewed my lip. Maybe Sarah could wait for five minutes while I crammed in a few bites. My mouth was already watering from the smell of curry and ginger. I grabbed my plate and scooped a heap onto my plate. I looked at my grandfather out of the corner of my eye and noticed him watching me intently.

"If you know him so well," I said to him. "Why has he never been here before?"

My grandfather had the grace to blush, but he went on undeterred. "Callum here never dared cross my threshold after *the incident*."

He said it with all the mystery of a taut thriller, and Callum groaned out loud in mock protest.

"I'm not sure I want to know," I said. "It sounds so dastardly."

"Oh," Gramp said. "It was. It really was." He shoveled in a forkful of peas and chewed around a half smile. It was obvious he wanted Callum to do the talking.

I shifted my gaze to the broad shouldered man sitting across from my grandfather. I almost didn't want to look at him fully. In my mind, he was still the dusty man who carried me out of the cathedral and accused me of arson. He was the man who followed me to the crypt because he was suspicious of me.

I didn't want to think of the man who had carried me out of that same crypt and swiped the tears from my cheek when I had broken down. I still carried the look of his eyes in my mind, and the way his black hair had turned grey from the dust. The stubble on his chin had carried the remnants of cobwebs.

It was far easier for my regular mindset to believe the worst. It had been proven right so many times, I'd be a fool not to heed it. I lifted my chin, watching for Callum's reaction, daring him to be anything but the same kind of person as those women from the night before who are always so ready to accuse me.

He watched me silently for a long moment, and I let the dare show in my gaze. I wasn't sure what reaction I wanted from him, maybe I was testing him the same as I had done Gramp for so many years. But whatever reaction I hoped for was not the one I received. Instead of responding to my inquisitive look with support, he dropped his fork back onto his plate and looked up at me.

I thought my heart might stop for a moment as those green eyes landed on me. I thought he might confess to me, bring me into his circle of trust. I held my breath as I waited.

"I don't want to talk about it," he said flatly, and in that moment, I knew that even after all we'd been through in the crypt, he still saw me as a kid.

I struggled to find the words to retaliate, and when they wouldn't come I dropped my plate onto the table and spun on my heel.

I shrugged into a jean jacket. The words stung. Almost as much as the way my calf burned where the brand had been set. Except this pain had struck me somewhere different. My throat ached with it.

"I'll be back later, Gramp."

Gramp stood with his fingers on the table top. I could see by his face that he was worried, that he wasn't sure how to ask me to stay home.

"I'm fine," I said, purposefully avoiding Callum's eye. "You don't have to worry."

"Ayla," Callum said, and I held up my hand.

"I'm fine," I insisted. "I'm going to see Sarah." I couldn't meet his gaze, couldn't even look at his hands as they fidgeted on the table, tapping the butt of his fork against the plate.

Instead I looked at Gramp. His eyes trailed down to the table and I thought for a moment he might argue with me. I didn't really want to have to defy him, but if Callum had told him everything then he would surely understand why I had to go. As usual, he surprised me.

"I have something for her," he said and followed me into the hallway, rustling through one of the drawers along the pass-through counter. He came out with a bag made of soft leather and tied with what looked like a root of some kind.

"What's this?"

He wouldn't look me in the eye as he put it into my hand. "She'll know what it is," he said.

I gave him a conspiratorial glance. "Is this pot?" I said, teasing. When he met my gaze I could see that he was worrying his lip with his top teeth.

"What's wrong?" I said.

He finally looked at me and his black eyes beneath those bushy silver eyebrows looked even more piercing than normal.

"If you can do anything for her, do it," he said. "But know what it is you're doing."

"How much did Callum tell you?"

"Enough to make me nervous," Gramp said.

I shook the bag in my hand. It didn't feel like it was full of anything at all. There were no marbles rolling around in it and it didn't feel as though there was anything as gritty as sand and yet it kept its shape as though it was blown up like a balloon.

Over his shoulder I could see Callum watching me and the sight of those green eyes made me flick my gaze back to Gramp because he looked too intent, as though he was going to grab me by the elbows and throw me against the wall. I squirmed uncomfortably at the thought of it because I wasn't sure whether I wanted him to do it or not. Even my throat ached when I looked at him.

"I'll take my scooter," I mumbled. "And I'll try not to be late. I'll call you from the hospital."

Gramp leaned down and planted a soft kiss on the top of my hair. "Such beautiful red hair," he murmured. "Just like your mother's."

He never spoke of mom. Neither did I. She was a silent partner in my tenure here. I knew if he mentioned her at all, he must be feeling more anxious than he wanted to admit. I threw my arms around him and hugged him tightly. The smell of his Old Spice aftershave washed over me. He made me feel safe and loved. I put everything I couldn't say to him into that embrace.

He kissed my ear. "Be careful."

I fled for the door because my eyes were burning and I didn't like the sound of a chair scraping against the tiles of the kitchen floor.

I yanked the door open and ran to my scooter. The air did wonders for the burning in my eyes. I pulled my helmet on and kicked the scooter to life.

It was a twenty minute ride to the hospital on Old Yeller because it didn't go as fast as Callum's little beater car. By the time I got there, I expected to see Sarah sitting up in bed or on a chair having supper. What greeted me when I made it to her room was an empty bed all made up. I blinked at it in confusion and then spun on my heel to find reception.

The young woman behind the counter wore her hair in a braided bun. I thought I could detect a lock of pink in the black. Soft looking blue eyes peered at me from beneath two little curls of hair sprayed into place against her temple. Her mouth made a perfect heart shape and it was even pencilled in at the edges to accentuate the fullness. I felt like a mangy rat crawling out of the gutter looking at her.

"Has Sarah been released?" I asked her.

That beautifully painted mouth pressed together and I thought she would refuse to answer. Instead, she lifted her pencil and pointed it toward the room Sarah had occupied. "You mean that girl?" she said in a voice that sounded like honey. Perfect match to the face. Encouraged, I nodded my head.

"Yes," I said. "We brought her in yesterday."

"You're family?"

What was one more lie? "Yes."

"Then you would know where she is," she said with a conspiratorial look on her face.

I clenched the counter with anxious fingers. I wasn't sure how to reply, what would make her spill the information and I was about to do something ridiculous when everything in her face softened and her shoulders sagged. A dreamy look came over her face as she looked over my shoulder.

I didn't need to turn around to know it was Callum but I did. All six feet four of him stood no more than a yard behind me. In the full light of the hospital it was clear exactly how magnificent he was all cleaned up. I hadn't wanted to see it back in Gramp's kitchen because I knew deep down the reason for the ache in my throat. I was attracted to him. I wanted him. And he thought I was nothing but a kid.

I felt him standing behind me.

"Where did they put her, Faye?" he said.

Whatever obligation had kept Faye from telling me where they had put Sarah, seemed to disappear in the face of Callum's brooding stature. Or maybe it was those piercing green eyes. Or it could be the way those rakish looks of his made a girl ignore her own instincts.

"This is official business, right?" she said but didn't wait for him to answer. "She's on the fourth floor."

One black eyebrow cocked and his mouth twitched. I saw a blush creep up Faye's neck under that look, and I wondered for a second if the two of them had known each other more intimately than either of them were letting on. It certainly seemed it by the way Faye was twisting her fingers together over the pencil.

"Fourth floor?" I said, taking in the way Faye had taken to leaning over the counter, the swell of her bosom visible over the starched white neck line of her uniform. "Why did they move her?"

I felt Callum move up next to me and had to struggle to remain in my spot without bolting away. I had just faced down a doppelgänger, for heaven sake. Surely I could stand next to him without turning to water.

It was obvious from Faye's face that she didn't like the way he stood just a little too close to me. I felt his shoulder brush against mine and I had the feeling that if I would look up, he would be towering over me with a glower on his face. I wrapped my fingers around the bag in my jean jacket pocket, reminding myself that I was here for a reason. And it had nothing to do with getting close to the brooding hulk next to me.

"What's the fourth floor?" I said.

Callum reached his hand across the counter and plucked the pencil from Faye's fingers. He pulled the clipboard across the counter and scribbled something down on the paper. Then he pushed it back at Faye.

"I'm the one that pulled her out of there," he said.

Faye nodded. "Everyone's talking about it," she said. "It'll be nice to know whether or not she set that fire."

She looked at me with a strange glint in her eye. "Isn't that Tulley's granddaughter?" She took the pencil back from Callum, and I noticed that her fingers trailed up his wrist as she did so. "I mean," she said, holding my gaze while talking to Callum. "Everyone figured it would be her. Who would've thought some stranger would do it?"

Callum shrugged but I noticed he didn't pull his hand away. For some reason, I couldn't tear my eyes from the way Faye's fingers still touched his fingertips against the counter.

I cleared my throat, maybe just a little too aggressively. When they both shot a look my way, I barked out one word. "Sarah."

Faye's entire demeanor changed then. She looked irritated. "Fourth floor, I said." Then she jerked her chin toward the elevators. "Mental health unit." I swallowed and squared my shoulders as I leveled her with a direct stare. "You look a lot nicer than you are," I said and twirled around.

I'd be damned if I'd thank her, but I noticed Callum did. And to top it off, he said something patronizing about me that sounded an awful lot like: she is a bit prickly. "Teenage hormones and all that," is what he said.

I fumed the entire way to the elevator and punched the buttons. I stood with my face lifted to the lights above the doors. And even when he came next to me, chuckling as though he had just heard a great joke, I refused to look at him. When the doors opened, I pushed inside and found my way into the corner.

He stood in the middle and reached out to press the button for the fourth floor. Then he stood there with his hands crossed over his hips. I thought I could detect a small smile playing at the corner of his mouth, and something burned deep in my chest.

"Teenage hormones?" I ground out.

He tapped his foot as though he was listening to some interesting music.

"Really?" I demanded.

He swung his head sideways to look at me. "You're pretty determined to screw things up, aren't you?" he said.

"What do you mean?" I said.

"I mean you get more flies with honey than with

vinegar."

I snorted. "I've heard that one never before."

"Well it's true," he said. "People have jobs to do and there are rules to those jobs sometimes. If you want people to give you information that you're not supposed to have, you really need to be nice."

"I was being nice," I said, stung.

One of his black brows cocked again. "That's you being nice? You might need a few lessons."

He was one to talk. I lurched closer so I could poke him in the chest. I seemed to recall a pretty bland refusal to be nice to me back at Gramp's.

"You might apply that stupid cliche to yourself," I said. I was vaguely aware my finger wasn't jamming into his chest very far.

As if to prove my suspicions, he tightened his pectoral muscles until they felt like steel bands. The next time I stabbed him, my knuckle bent sideways painfully. I hastily retracted my hand and shoved it in my jeans pocket. A revoltingly arrogant smile twisted his lips. He made a face that was very clearly an expression meant to goad me into daring to do it again. I dug my hands into my pockets. I hated how he made me feel so young and awkward.

"I was embarrassed," he said finally. "Back at the house. It was an embarrassing story. That's why I didn't want to tell you."

"I don't care," I muttered. But of course, I did. I just wasn't ready to let him know it meant anything to me.

He made a little grumbling noise, muttering something

about me being difficult and hard to be nice to.

"Oh because Faye isn't hard to be nice to," I said, feeling a bright bit of fury sinking into my chest.

He peered down at me. "I've known her a long time."

"I guessed that." I snorted. I definitely didn't want to know that.

"You're jealous," he said. I would've expected him to sound surprised or at the very least shocked. But it was a bald statement that somehow found a way to make my chest hurt.

"I'm not jealous," I said. I crossed my arms over my chest.

"I'm at least three years older than you," he said. "I know jealousy when I see it."

I twisted away from him to look at the lights over the door. The elevator had to be a century-old it was so slow. We were only on number three. The elevator stopped and the doors opened. No one was there.

I thought my silence would give him the hint but it didn't.

"What do you want from me, Ayla?"

This time I managed to look at him, and as the doors pulled open at the fourth floor, I faced them with the same direct and bald-faced stare I had given Faye. I didn't care that his expression was pleading and soft and he looked so darned gorgeous it made my tongue feel all tied up and clumsy.

"I want you to leave me alone," I blurted out and then because I couldn't believe I'd said something so awful, so completely childish, I bolted out the elevator and ran down the hallway even though I had no idea which direction I should be going.

CHAPTER 13

He caught up with me in a few easy strides, testament to how quick he was, how long those legs were. Instead of snagging me by the elbow and spinning me around, he swerved around me and put his hand out against the wall, effectively blocking my way unless I dodged around him.

"You're going the wrong way," he drawled.

There was a smirk on his face that I dearly wanted to slap off. I even pulled my fist back, clenching my fingers with every intent to let him have it. Instead of punching him, I ended up slapping him on the chest with the flat of my hand. Frustrated, and feeling very inept for as furious as I was.

"You said she would be sedated so she could sleep," I accused him.

"That's what I thought," he said. "She was exhausted. Spent. They were going to put fluids in her as far as I understood."

"Well now she's in some psych unit and it's all your fault. I swear, if she's in a strait jacket..."

"It's not my fault," he said stressing that last word. "She needed medical care. You couldn't have just brought her home and expected her to do well. She needed to see a doctor."

"Well now the doctor has put her at risk. You heard her say she wasn't safe here. What if one of those things finds her? What then? You remember what we went through."

I sidestepped him, fully intending to pass by until I remembered I was going the wrong way. That was when I felt his arm snake out and wrap around my midriff. He pulled me unceremoniously to his side and then pushed me roughly behind his back. His other arm reached around to catch my arm. Pinned, I fumed and struggled to find a way out of his grasp.

"Stay still," he hissed.

"What is it?" I said. I tried to twist in his grip and peek around his shoulder, but he was as broad as a wall and about as movable.

"Sarah," he said. "Tell me that's Sarah." He took a small side step, pulling me out from behind him at the same time so that I could peer up the hallway. As I craned my way around him, I could feel how tense the muscles were in his biceps. He was on guard, wary. But it was her. Thank the gods. I was so relieved to see her, it didn't register that she was supposed to be in a ward room with another patient. And there she stood, not in a hospital gown as I expected, but fully dressed.

"Sarah," I said. I felt hopeful in the moment. "Are they letting you out?"

She said nothing. Just blinked at me.

I felt Callum tug me back into his chest. I came up hard against it as though it was a solid brick wall, and I had to put my hands out. My palms brushed down his biceps and they quivered beneath my hands.

"It's not Sarah," he hissed.

I understood right then. The doppelgänger. Here. At first, I wanted to bolt down the hall, but as I watched it, I noticed it wasn't attacking. That didn't mean it wouldn't.

"What are we going to do?" I said and pushed myself away from him. The only thing that kept me from tearing down the hall was Callum firm grip on my hand.

Everything in my body just sort of clenched in fear, but there was something else too and I should have noticed it when we entered the hallway from the elevator. That tingling in my ears. The whistling that sounded as though it was coming from some deep bowel in the earth. But I had been so preoccupied with arguing with Callum, I'd not noticed it. Now that I had, I had no idea how I had let it pass over me unnoticed.

"I'm not ready," I heard myself say. I knew this was the moment when I had to do something.

Obviously, we'd not killed it back there in the tunnel. Obviously, Sarah hadn't been able to do anything more than send it laughing somewhere back to its master, whoever that was. If the doppelgänger was here, then she really wasn't safe. And based on what it had done to us back in the tunnel, neither was anyone else.

"I have to do something," I said and shook myself free of his grip.

"But it's not moving, Ayla," Callum said. "Maybe Sarah did damage to it. Maybe it doesn't have the strength to hurt us."

"Or maybe it's taunting me. Or maybe it has already harmed her and is waiting for us to find out."

Easing forward, my hands in front of me as though in surrender, I started talking to it the way one might a rabid dog. Maybe it would let me pass. Callum snagged me around the waist and stepped up next to me, his arm lying across my chest as though to shield me.

"That's not smart, Ayla."

"You know what it did to you last time," I said through gritted teeth. "How are you going to stop it?"

"Because I'm ready for it this time," he said.

I sent harried glances around us. We couldn't fight that thing in the hallway. What if no one else saw it but us? In the end if we did anything, no doubt we'd be tossed out on our ears and Sarah would be left here alone with it.

"What do you want?" I asked of it.

It merely smiled at me with a snakelike grin that stretched across his face in an eerie yet calm movement.

In that moment, a nurse exited from Sarah's ward room and brushed through the space where the doppelgänger stood. It disappeared like smoke and I felt as though a cold blast of wind had swept across my face. I shivered. Hugged myself with my arms crossed over my chest.

"Did that make you as nauseous as it did me?" I murmured.

"If you mean do I feel as though I just had a chance to get a really good whiff of death's armpits," Callum said. "Then yes."

"Then that clinches it," I said, looking up at him and let the relief show on my face. He touched my chin with his thumb and then pulled it away as if he'd not meant to touch me at all.

I looked at the space the thing had been. "It's not strong enough. Whatever she did to it back there, it's drained."

Both of us converged on Sarah's room so quickly, that we met the doorway at the same time. He was so broad, however, he took up most of the space and I ended up having to squeeze past him when I saw Sarah lying in her bed. She was hooked up to an IV, sleeping.

I crept up next to the bed and lay my hand on hers. She still looked pale but not as ghastly white as she had when we left the crypt. There was indeed one other person in the room with her, fiddling with her cell phone. I ignored the girl when she gave me an annoyed look and sat down next to Sarah. Callum flicked the curtain closed around us. The metallic clang of stainless steel rings against stainless steel rods met my ears. I waited until we were enclosed in the curtain before I lay a hand on her forehead, stroking the black bangs away from her eyes.

I was relieved when they fluttered open.

"Sarah," I said in a breath. "How are you doing?"

I was relieved to see she wasn't in a strait jacket, but merely lay quietly in the bed. The sheets were tucked up to her collarbone and her arms lay outside them on the sheets. Tubes and wires ran everywhere. She looked at me without recognition at first.

"Chemical restraints," Callum said. "They're keeping her quiet with drugs."

"Shit," I said. I tried to imagine what it would feel like to be powerless and trapped in my body and shivered. "How is this safe for her?"

I stared down and noticed her mouth working to speak.

I pressed my ear against her mouth.

"What?" I said when I felt her lips move but heard nothing.

There was a moment when the tinnitus in my ear got so loud, I thought perhaps she had screeched into it and I flinched, pulling away from her without meaning to. It was then that I realized Callum had thrown himself onto the bed and was pushing me away from it. His shove sent me reeling back into the curtain and I grabbed the material to keep from falling.

There, standing next to her bed, was the doppelgänger. It smiled very prettily, sweeping blonde hair away from its cheek and tucking it behind a duplicate of Sarah's delicate ear. Without a word, it sat down next to her on the bed and twirled a lock of her black hair around its finger. Pulled it out straight and then twirled around its finger again. All the while, it watched me as I stood paralyzed. I was vaguely aware that Callum had stepped behind me and that his arm was around my waist. I could feel his breath sweeping across the top of my head. For a second, I felt claustrophobic. The electric jolt of his touch firing off alarms in my tissues at the same time as the buzzing in my ears made me feel as though the room was closing in on me. I clutched at my chest, trying to remind myself my heart was still beating.

"What in the hell is it doing here?" he whispered in my ear. I had the feeling he was hoping that thing couldn't hear us and at the same time was quite certain it could read lips.

I shook my head. "I have no idea. But I can't just let it sit there with her."

As if to confirm that it knew exactly what we were thinking, it lifted a finger and beckoned me closer. Fat chance of that. If anything, I was going to find something to throw at it. It smiled. Then it put the duplicate of Sarah's palm on the unconscious Sarah's head. I watched as my friend's mouth opened and a sound just sort of hissed out of it without her lips forming words.

"I know what you are," it said, then let go a derisive snort from Sarah's mouth. The effect the sound made as it moved from her lungs as someone played with her vocal cords wasn't near as awful as the way her expression remained perfectly clean of emotion. Both made my skin crawl. The buzzing in my ears intensified to a growl. The tattoo on my calf ached as though someone was twisting the skin. I had to reach out for the bed to keep myself from collapsing beneath the pain of it.

I felt Callum's hands spasm on my waist and I swallowed slowly, trying to form some response. I hated that it had managed to goad me, to frighten me.

"I know what *you* are," I said to it. "And I don't care."

I hoped it would get the message--that I had no plans to attack it. Heck. I didn't think I even could hurt it. I certainly hadn't been able to do so in the crypt the night before, and I was no better equipped today than I was yesterday.

Kill or incapacitate is what Sarah had said of it. I'd accepted the explanation at the time without question, because I was still trying to process all of the information coming at me at the speed of light. But now that the thing was in front of me again, toying with Sarah's hair, I found myself wondering exactly what powers it had been imbued it with. What its purpose was. She had dug herself into that crypt for a reason. She had carried with her a cooler of viscera and a few sandwiches and lit candles and lived there for at least a week before she texted me. I hadn't questioned any of that then. I questioned it now.

Whatever she was running from, it had to be worse than this. And this was pretty bad.

The thing seemed to watch every thought cross my mind. It cocked its head back and forth from one side to the next and then finally angled its head so that those bright blue eyes so much like Sarah's took me in like lamplight. A smile tugged at the corners of its mouth.

"You're still new," it mused from Sarah's mouth. "Fledgling." It stood to its feet and pulled its fingers down along Sarah's throat and shoulder and let them whisper all the way down her bare arm to her fingers. "How delightful."

I halted. It seemed to be growing more solid as we watched, gaining power. No doubt from its connection to Sarah. In no time, it might have enough to come at us again. Or to harm her. I was just three steps away and I could lunge forward if I wanted, but I'd seen what it could do in the blink of an eye back in the crypt. I knew it could transform into something far more terrifying with long fingers and a strength that could strangle with one hand. It could slip that hand around Sarah's neck and choke the life from her while we watched. Then it would be Callum and I in here with her with no way to explain how a girl could choke to death without either one of us touching her.

I tried to make eye contact with her, to see if she was aware of what was going on. Her eyes were opened, yes, but there was a vacant sort of look in them, as though the drugs were paralysing her and keeping her from processing anything she saw. Maybe that was a good thing. I held my hand out, nonthreatening.

It lunged at me, but never took its hand from Sarah's. Even so, I flinched and jumped backward, landing solidly into Callum.

"I don't think it wants to attack you," he whispered. "I think he's just trying to scare you."

"He?" I said. "You think it's trans?" It was a bad joke,

and I knew it, but I was too deep into the mucky pit of fear to rationalize whether or not it made sense. My fingers gripped the curtain, pulling the edges into my fist nervously.

"What do you think we should do?" I said.

"I say kill the bastard," Callum said.

The doppelgänger grinned.

"I think that's a dare," I said. I scrambled mentally for a way to do exactly what Callum suggested. Surely in a hospital room, there was more to hand than just a bedpan and a curtain.

"I've never passed up a dare yet," Callum said and even as he lunged for the thing, I grabbed his elbow.

"Not yet," I said. "We have no idea what it will do to Sarah. We don't even know how to kill it."

"I say we start with the throat and work our way through to the spine." He ground out.

I knew he was remembering exactly how he felt back in the crypt, surprised and powerless beneath the Doppelgängers grip. I understood exactly how he felt, but we simply didn't know enough to go on the offensive just yet.

"I'd feel better if it wasn't sitting so close to her when we try to...kill it." I wanted to believe it was for her safety, but something in the back of my mind reminded me of what I'd suffer if we succeeded--I didn't think I'd want to end up lying there in chemical restraints when the staff found me screaming in pain as a brand seared itself magically onto my skin.

"Maybe we can lure it away from her," I said.

I looked sideways at him to see his jawline rigid and tight with fury.

Callum took a step toward the bed but the thing didn't so much as move. It certainly wasn't threatened by a six foot four muscled fireman. At least it didn't lunge for us. I took a step forward, thinking maybe I could get his attention and draw it away from Sarah.

The thing hissed.

"Well, I'll be," Callum said. "It doesn't like you."

I leveled my gaze on the thing that looked like Sarah. "Feeling is mutual, dude," I said.

I wasn't sure what was holding it back, what was keeping it tethered to its place, but I was grateful for it. The curtains certainly didn't provide much security, and even with Callum standing right there, I was worried for the safety of the other patient. I wondered briefly if she heard us whispering about killing things behind the curtain, then I realized she'd been wearing her ear buds when we came in the room. But what of the nurses down the hallway? What if they came in and heard us? What if the thing decided to attack them?

We had to act quickly.

"Leave her alone," I said to it, hoping it would at least get distracted. "She told us exactly what you are. She told us exactly how to get rid of you." It was a ridiculous risk, but I didn't know what else to do.

It stole a glance over at the semiconscious girl in the bed. "She did?" It said through Sarah's lips.

I had the feeling it was glaring at her. I wasn't sure what powers the thing had. For all I knew, it could simply scoop her up and pop off into some other reality. I wasn't even sure if the thing was sitting there like a beacon for her family to hone in on. It had proven incredibly strong and dangerous in the crypt, and I couldn't put the rest of these innocent people at risk should it gather enough power to gain physical form.

"Yes, she did," I said. "She told us all about you."

"Is that a threat, Nathelium?" it said through Sarah's open mouth.

"Na--what?" Callum said. "Is it speaking English?"

"You're running out of time," It said through Sarah's mouth. Corporeality. It was gaining corporeality every second.

I expected the thing to hurl itself at me, and when it swung his gaze back around to face me, it had transformed just enough so that Sarah's beautiful face looked like that troll thing we'd encountered in the crypt. I thought it was trying to bully me. I didn't take well to bullying. Before I could give it a second thought, I stepped forward. As I did, the thing stepped back, leaning away from me as though we were two sides of one magnet.

"It doesn't want you anywhere near it," Callum said from behind me.

I knew it was true even as I took another step. The thing seemed to be forced backward. I leaned forward, it leaned backward. I cocked my head at it. I didn't think it was afraid of me. It certainly hadn't been the night before, so something was different.

The girl coughed from the other side of the curtain. Then she started into a coughing fit. I had the feeling she was going to press her buzzer and the nurses would be in at any moment. I was sure they wouldn't want to see the curtains around Sarah closed, wouldn't want to see someone in here at all. I jammed my hands into my pockets, searching for my phone so I could pretend I needed privacy to call a loved one.

My fingers brushed against something soft.

That was when I realized what was different about me today than yesterday. I yanked the bag Gramp had given me from my pocket and dangled it in front of me. In the very second I did that, the thing hissed and transformed so that Sarah's beautiful visage turned into something drawn and haggard.

A bubble of giddiness tripped its way up my throat. That was it. Whatever Gramp had given me for Sarah, this thing was repelled by it. I waved it forward as a test, and for every inch I moved it in the doppelgänger's direction, the doppelgänger leaned that far back.

"I'll be damned," Callum said from behind me.

I took one look at Sarah lying there on the bed with that thing's hand touching her skin and I threw the bag onto her chest. My moment of victory as it landed on Sarah's chest was short-lived. I hadn't counted on the doppelgänger being free to attack me if I wasn't holding the bag. It leapt for me. I had less than a second to react, and I knew my reflexes were too slow even on a good day. I also knew it had what it needed to lunge and do damage.

Callum pushed me from behind onto Sarah's bed and even as I twisted around on it to see what was going on behind me, I caught sight of that thing lifted off the floor and flying toward Callum. With not so much as a change of expression, his hand snapped forward and caught that beast straight in the throat. One twirl and leg kick later, Callum had connected it with the back of his heel. As the doppelgänger fell sideways, Callum's fingers jammed forward and the thing opened its mouth to let go a silent howl. Then it leveled its clouded gaze at me, one eye socket oozing yellow fluid and the other looking as though something had clotted inside behind the lens.

Sarah's chest lurched upward, her chest arching in what looked like a painful spasm. I watched horrified as the doppelgänger spoke through her again, this time letting her mouth move when she spoke.

"I bet you don't even know what he is," It said in a hoarse voice that could have been gravel running over chalkboard. Sarah took to laughing with a throaty chuckle that sounded so far from her regular feminine tinkle. It made my skin crawl.

"I do know," I said. "He's human. Just like me."

The thing gave me one last meaningful look. Then it disappeared.

I collapsed onto the bed, drained of every ounce of energy. I thought I could hear the other patient complaining on the other side of the curtain to stop all the noise. Then she swore. The next thing I knew, she was threatening to get the nurse.

I lifted my gaze to Callum's face. He could have gotten hurt. That thing could've killed him. If it had gotten hold of him, if it had managed to get close enough, things might have turned out very differently.

Even so, I had to give the guy credit. He'd stepped up. While I'd been frozen in fear with my slow reflexes, he'd done what I should have. Some grim reaper I turned out to be. I almost smiled, relieved I didn't have some preternatural abilities that would mark me as what Azrael claimed I had become. I almost laughed with relief.

"That was something," I said. "Think you can teach me to do that?"

He swayed in front of me for all of three seconds before he smiled.

Then he collapsed to his knees.

He was only then that I noticed the doppelgänger had somehow razored through his collarbone. A bloom of blood stained the front of his shirt.

I might have jumped from the bed to call for help, but apparently the noise had already done that for me.

The nurse flicked the curtain open and when she saw Callum on the floor and the blood pooling out from beneath him, all hell literally broke loose.

CHAPTER 14

I waited in the emergency room for three hours before I saw Callum again. I paced and flipped through magazines without seeing a single word. I turned on the television and snapped it off again because *Supernatural* was on and I didn't even want to think the word let alone watch a show filled with the stuff.

I was loathe to leave Sarah alone, and I hated Callum was somewhere behind the swinging doors where I couldn't see him. But I knew that if the doppelgänger had been repelled by the thing Gramp had sent for her, that tucked beneath her pillow, it should keep her safe enough till I returned.

That didn't mean we were safe. I had to take it on faith the thing wouldn't show itself in a room full of doctors. That it would hover around Sarah but be unable to hurt her.

I had no idea what was in the little satchel Gramp had

given me, but if it was enough to repel a beast like that, then I resolved to ask him for a dozen of them.

By the time Callum did come out of the triage room with a bright white bandage peeking out from beneath his shirt and a red stain covering him from collar to midchest, I was tired and hungry and about ready to claw my way through the nurse who ushered him out into the waiting room.

"About time," I said grumpily. I didn't want to ask how he was. I was afraid of his answer.

He gave me a sheepish, yet surprised grin. "I didn't expect to see you here," he said.

I pushed off the plastic chair and took a step toward him, uneasy, tentative. I jammed my hands into my jacket pocket because I had no idea what to do with them.

"Well I couldn't just leave you here," I said. "You still have to tell me how you did that."

"And here I thought you cared," he said.

I chewed my lip. "I do," I said. "I mean, it's just that..."

For some reason, my hands in my pockets turned my jacket into some strangely winged bird flapping about. When I realized how ridiculous I must look, I pulled my hands free of the pockets and stuck them beneath my armpits, hugging myself and toeing the floor with the tip of my boot.

I could barely look at him.

"So you're going to be okay?" I asked from beneath the fringe of my bangs.

"Just needed a few stitches. Apparently the thing bit

me just as I jabbed my fingers in its eyes."

Impressive. Not something I would've thought of doing.

"About that..." I started to say, knowing that what should follow was a thank you, but I was having a tough time getting it past my tongue. Had he not acted fast, that thing would have razored through me, and I doubted I would have been as lucky as he was. The expression 'dead as a door nail' took a little jaunt through my mind.

Something shivered down my spine as I remembered Azrael telling me that this life would be my last if I didn't earn my wings. As a regular human being, at least I would've had the hope of heaven or some afterlife. But if I was what Azrael said I was, I'd end up in the top of his cane for ever more.

That meant I really owed Callum.

He must've been watching me struggling because while I was zoned out with my thoughts, he had somehow crept closer. He towered over me and looked down at me with those glassy green eyes and his gaze didn't look angry or accusatory. It just looked contemplative.

"Say it," he said with half a grin that was just big enough to make my belly flip-flop.

I let go a long sigh. "Thank you," I said. "No one has done anything like that for me before. At least no one except Gramp."

One step closer and he would be near enough that I would smell the soap on him again, maybe even feel his breath on my hair. I leaned in. Chewed at the bottom of my lip. He seemed to be waiting for something and I couldn't imagine what it was now that I had given him his thank you. What else could he want?

I fidgeted and finally broke away. The least he could've done was accept the thanks. What was with this horrible tension? It could make a girl crazy.

I spun to face away from him, fully intending to make my way back to Sarah's room. Maybe she would be awake by now. Maybe I could put this whole entire thing into perspective once I got a chance to talk to her.

I got three steps away when I felt his fingers tangle in mine. I half expected to be tugged backwards, but instead I was spun around and in one broad step, he was right there again, standing over me, looking down at me with a strange look on his face. Those black brows of his were furrowed and his eyes seemed to be looking straight through me.

"That's not what I wanted you to say," he whispered.

Before I could reply, his mouth was on mine, parting my lips softly, inhaling my breath. A jolt went straight down through my spine and something in my chest lurched like it was flipping over. I had two seconds or so to respond, but before I could, his mouth left mine and he drew away.

For one long moment, both of us stood there looking at each other.

"Your first kiss?" he said.

"Of course not," I said, feeling foolish. I might have told him that I'd kissed plenty of boys in my day, initiated plenty. But how could I say that moment was the first time I had kissed a man. His touch had been soft, but it had been commanding. There had been no hesitation in it. It wanted more, that kiss, no matter how gentle it had been. My lips were still tingling from it.

"Maybe it shocked you then," he said, and it was a playful tone that I wasn't used to. I felt awkward and silly. And I hated that I felt inexperienced and clumsy.

"Maybe you just weren't good at it." I said, before I could stop myself.

He immediately went all rigid. Of course he would. I might as well have shoved a knife in his belly. I wished I could take it back. I tried to reach for his hand, to make some physical contact because my mouth and my mind didn't seem to work in concert at all, and I hoped touching him might say the things I couldn't.

He brushed my hand away.

"It's time to go home anyway," he said. "Visiting hours are over and there's no way they're going to let us back in."

I stood there like an idiot watching him storm down the hallway toward the lobby. My fingers found my lips and I ran my thumb across them, trying to remember what his mouth felt like. Trying to work out how I felt about it because no matter what I had said, he was most definitely good at it.

I watched him until he disappeared through the front doors. I thought he might turn around, but he didn't. The glass sliding doors whispered shut and I stood there blinking like a dumbfounded fool, telling myself that no matter how many times I insisted I was an adult, I was very much a child in that moment.

Instead of enjoying the kiss, of savouring it the way I knew I would have wanted to had I been prepared for it , I had let my insecurities ruin it for me. And now he thought I wasn't interested in him. Worse than that, he thought I was repulsed by his kiss. I felt desolate in that moment because I didn't know how to fix it.

I pulled out my cell phone, thinking to text him. But what would I say? And would he even care? If it were me on the other end of that message, I would press delete. No doubt he would do the same. I stared down at the screen, running my thumb along the edge of the phone. There was nothing I could do and yet I didn't know how to stop staring at the message icon. I ended up flipping through the messages, and since there weren't many, I landed on Sarah's within seconds. Maybe that would help. I had no idea if it would work, but I had to do something to stop thinking about him. If it meant sneaking back into see her to distract my mind, so be it.

I made it as far as the nurse's station before I was shooed back out. I threw a look over my shoulder, but didn't see the doppelgänger at all. I hoped it was a good sign. I hoped that whatever my grandfather had given me was working. More than that, I didn't know what it was capable of.

It occurred to me that whatever that bag had been filled with, I had the original creator living with me.

I hopped onto my scooter feeling strangely buoyant

and invigorated.

The fall air felt divine against my face, and focusing on the ride in the traffic rewired my thoughts. I found myself thinking about Callum again. No matter how fast I went on the scooter, I couldn't get rid of the feel of his tongue pressed against mine, of the taste of his breath.

I pulled into my grandfather's driveway less than twenty minutes later. The sky was already darkening but it hung on to the last bit of light the way a dying man might the end of the rope. The shadows of trees along the driveway looked like gnarled fingers stretching forward to wrap around his little bungalow.

I kicked the motor off and propped it against the garage. I knew better than to try and stuff it inside, because although it was a garage, my grandfather had every derelict piece of furniture and abandoned piece of paper his fingers had ever touched in there. It had become a sanctuary for mice and raccoons and I'd learned long ago not to even bother opening the door.

Instead, I crossed my arms over my chest, taking in the house and feeling for the first time in a long time that I was grateful. I'd never had a true home, not with my mother or father since they moved from apartment to apartment all over the country, chasing gigs in seedy bars as my father tried to make it big as a guitar god. My mother followed him without question, and dragged me along. When they died in a car accident coming home from one of those gigs, we were so far across the country and so far removed from family that I didn't even know if I had any relatives left.

Foster care had been a nightmare that I barely woke from to find a little bit of light now and again. At the time, Sarah had been one of the only bits of illumination in a very dark midnight.

Now, looking at the house I called home, I knew I would never again do anything to jeopardize what I had here. I felt a smile playing across my lips. It felt good to be here in Dyre with Gramp. It felt right.

With a contented sigh, I strolled across the lawn and pushed the front door open. I called out for Gramp, even though I imagined he was sitting in front of the television with a cup of cocoa in his hand and his dogeared copy of Moby Dick in the other.

And although I imagined both of those things, I knew he wouldn't be paying attention to either of them. He'd be waiting for me, making sure everything was alright and that things were good between us before he went to bed. Like he had every night since I'd arrived four years ago.

I was closing the door behind me when I saw him in the hallway. He looked fresh and bright and terribly well rested for a man who probably hadn't caught ten minutes of sleep in the last 24 hours.

"I guess your bag worked," I said, peeling the jacket off my shoulders and hanging it on the coat rack. "What was in that thing anyway?"

He leaned against the wall next to the pass-through counter and crossed one ankle over the other. I noticed his feet were bare. A strange thing for him because he always had those Birkenstocks shoved onto his feet from morning till night. I always sort of suspected he slept in them.

I looked sideways at the pass-through counter, half expecting to see two mugs of cocoa sitting on the table in the kitchen, and as I did so, a strange little quiver ran down my spine. Something was off. I couldn't put my finger on it, but as I walked toward the kitchen, tilting my head so I could see, I knew things weren't quite right.

"Gramp?" I said, testing.

He didn't move, rather he just stood there, watching me.

It wasn't the empty table that caught my attention--not at first--although it certainly registered somewhere in the back of my consciousness. It was the pot that sat lopsided off the burner on the stove. I sniffed. I couldn't detect any gas. The burner wasn't fired. But there was something strange about the way that pot sat, lopsided, between the two gas racks.

My gaze snapped back to my grandfather.

"What was in the bag, Gramp?" I asked him again, this time firm and commanding. I cocked my head, listening for a buzzing in my ear. Nothing.

"Gramp?"

I heard a moan coming from somewhere beyond the counter. I looked again at Gramp as he stood there watching me. One eyebrow cocked, and for a second he looked as though he was waiting for me to comprehend what was going on. It was almost as if he wanted to ask me why in the hell I hadn't made the connection yet.

Doppelgänger.

I froze, trying to work out the timeliness in my mind. Trying to decide whether or not Gramp was here in the house, why the thing would have left Sarah to come all the way here when it couldn't possibly know Gramp had been the one who had made whatever was in that bag. It was somewhere between the thing's shuffling movement as it hopped up onto the counter and me dropping my helmet onto the floor that I realized it wasn't the same doppelgänger. This one didn't look threatening. He looked almost like the better and deeper thing that Gramp was. Playful. Brooding. It wasn't Sarah's doppelgänger. Not by a long shot.

But I knew that underneath that facade, there was something horrible.

I almost backed away and ran for the stairs, thinking I could run to warn Gramp, but I heard a moan again coming from the kitchen. That was when I realized he was on the other side of it, probably lying on the floor. He must have fallen. No doubt in the middle of making his cocoa. And now that thing was sitting there watching me. It could only mean one thing.

The realization of why it was there was enough to propel me through the hallway. The doppelgänger jumped down from the counter and without thinking I barreled through, heading for Gramp, busting through its facade as though it was nothing but smoke. An icy wind blew through me as I ran right through it. And the buzzing came then, screeching through my ears loud enough that if I hadn't been in such a panic, I would've stopped them up with my palms.

I skidded to a stop next to my grandfather on the floor.

He was lying face down.

I thought I saw blood coming out of his ears. I felt my breath suck in, and horrified, I searched for a pulse. I couldn't think. My mind just sort of froze and when it did it slipped into a groove that did not help.

Stroke. Aneurysm. His brain had exploded.

Any and all of those things were possible in the moment. I yanked my cell phone out of my pocket and jabbed at the numbers that would send an ambulance screaming to my house. I gave them the details. Somehow, I was rational enough to explain what he looked like. That he was breathing. Just barely.

The doppelgänger appeared again on the other side of the kitchen. I threw my cell phone at it and it wavered for a second, warping into its original shape and then back into the facade of my grandfather. It opened its mouth and for a horrible second I thought it would talk through my unconscious Gramp like the other one had with Sarah. I wasn't about to give it a chance.

I yelled at it. "Shut up. Shut up. Don't you dare say a word."

I realized in that second that I really understood what the presence of the doppelgänger meant. Harbinger of death. Warning of impending doom. I could sit there and howl over my grandfather's body and do nothing, or I could do something. Anything. I wasn't going to just sit there and let him die. I was going to fight for him. And I was going to win.

I rolled him over onto his back as gently as I could and I tilted his head back, propping it the way I had learned in one of those insufferable first aid classes they made us take in school. I listened for his breath. Felt for his pulse. Thready, both of them. But there. From over his chest I could see the doppelgänger shiver closer. It crouched on the other side of him and watched me. I should've been terrified with that thing giving me such intent study; I should have been so soaked with adrenaline and fear that I was all but useless, but all I could think of was losing Gramp. And that was not going to happen today.

"You're not taking him," I said to it. "I don't know what kind of payload you get from sitting around watching people die, but you can't have this one."

I clenched my fists together and came down hard on Gramp's chest, and then I planted my palms beneath his sternum. Pumped once twice three times.

I glanced sideways at my grandfather's face, trying to assess whether or not he was coming to. The doppelgänger had shifted and was now squatting at the top of his head. It caught my eye and then looked down at my grandfather's face. For a second, I thought it was going to touch him.

"Get away from him," I yelled.

Pumped again. One two three..Thirty. Breathe into his mouth. Breathe again.

The doppelgänger got to his feet and strolled around the perimeter of Gramp's body. It brushed through me, making my ears buzz and sending a wash of frigid air across my skin. Then it broke on the other side and I felt nauseous. Sweat broke out across my brow. But I couldn't stop. I pumped. Breathed. Pumped again.

An eternity died before I heard the sirens in the distance. A shudder racked through me and I couldn't tell if it was fear, relief, or terror. Even as the siren grew louder and wailed with an even keener note, I knew I was losing him. The pulse was less strong. The breaths were nothing but a sigh when they came at all.

"Please, Gramp," I sobbed. My shoulders ached. Each thrust seemed to have less and less energy. I thought I would collapse over his body and that would be the last of it. We'd both be found there, nothing left of us but shells.

I looked up over his chest to see the doppelgänger again. It was squatting with its arms crossed over its knees. Leaning over. Inspecting my work. I got the feeling he was thinking that its time was almost done. That it saw what it needed to in Gramp's face and would soon be finished its little job and would move on to the next.

"Bastard," I said to it. It occurred to me I might try to attack it like I had the one in the crypt, but I didn't dare stop. You never stopped. That was the only thing I really remembered from the classes. Don't stop until the paramedics get there. Not until someone else takes over.

"You knew I wouldn't be able to attack you," I yelled at it.

Even as I said the words, I realized how ridiculous they sounded. This thing had no power to kill. It wasn't a reaper. It was a simple doppelgänger. Even Sarah had said hers had been empowered by her coven in order to gain the sort of power it had. There would be no reason for her coven to give that sort of power to this one. They didn't even know about us. They couldn't, and so I knew they couldn't have sent this thing.

This thing had simply come because my grandfather was dying. I sobbed out loud. It was hopeless. I swore that if I managed to get him through, I would find out whatever I had to so this wouldn't happen again. I wouldn't be powerless while someone I loved died in front of me.

It occurred to me that this thing had tried to warn me. That's what it had been doing when it showed itself to me. I realized it didn't want him to die. It was simply doing its job. Warning of doom.

"Well, you got it wrong, buddy," I said to it. And I pumped again. One to three. Breathe. Felt for a pulse.

I stole a glance at it as I breathed into my grandfather's mouth. The thing shivered for second. Then solidified. It lost Gramp's facade and it leered at me in its true form. I thought I saw it bare its teeth like a cornered cat might. Angry. Threatened.

"I've got your number now," I said to it. "You better believe I've got your number."

With great deliberation, I pulled my gaze from the doppelgänger and paid attention to my grandfather. I pumped in earnest now. Worked at his chest and breathed for him. The sirens drew ever closer and the wail of it was so loud I knew they were pulling into the driveway. It didn't matter. I wouldn't stop now.

They were breaking into the door when I heard my grandfather gasp in a draft of air. I leaned back on my haunches as the paramedics bustled around me. I heard them talking about just in time. They got to him just in time. Good thing I was here.

I nodded, mutely, stupidly. I didn't need to be told. I knew things had shifted the moment I felt the doppelgänger rise to its feet. As they pulled my grandfather onto a stretcher and wheeled him down the hallway, I watched the doppelgänger shrivel into a desiccated looking creature. Its mouth gaped open and closed.

Gasping for air, I thought.

My grandfather's life was this thing's death. I almost laughed at the ease of it. It had been nothing like what the maniac had done to me in the cathedral. There were no incantations. No holy oil. I simply had to keep my grandfather from giving into the doom that the creature was foretelling.

It didn't turn into glittery dust like the maniac in the church had. Instead, it collapsed to its knees, clutching its throat. It was a bit anticlimactic to see it fall onto its side and lie there, twitching. Even so, I waited. If the episode in the church had taught me anything, it was what would come next.

And it did. Mere moments later. Twisting agony branded itself onto my rib cage and brought me to my knees.

CHAPTER 15

I was outraged both at the pain and at the thought that there was no way I'd be able to follow the ambulance to the hospital while I was hunched over, clutching my rib cage with a fierce grip because I could barely breathe through the pain. It seared through me, twisting the muscles between my ribs as the brand worked its way through my tissues.

I was gasping and panting for air when I saw the silver tip of cane appear on the floor in front of me. The silver tip moved in and out of my vision as it tapped against the linoleum floor. Whoever held onto it was trying desperately to get my attention.

I looked up to see Azrael looking incredibly out of place in the 70s style kitchen. He looked nothing like the old man I'd last met and instead appeared as the gorgeous, pale skinned man he'd let me glimpse back in the cathedral. Far too beautiful to be real, and yet I knew he was. He had shed the facade of the old man with red wool socks and Birkenstocks. Instead, he let me see that lush charcoal hair again and that blue eyed gaze that could've been hard chunks of ice if they weren't so alive and vibrant. He looked for all the world like a Wall Street investment banker might look, complete with pinstriped suit and narrow red tie.

My gaze flicked from him to the shriveled pile of desiccated flesh on the floor in front of me. I lurched over to a chair, and pushed my bottom onto the seat. I had to grip the back of the chair to keep from falling off it again as I found solid seating. Bile rose to my cheeks and I had to swallow it down past a burning in my throat just to choke out a few words.

I knew why he was here. And I wasn't happy about it.

"I don't have time for this," I managed to cough out before another spasm twisted through my ribs.

The tip of his cane tapped closer.

"There's no need to worry about the old man," he said. "The death of his doppelgänger indicates he's going to be just fine."

"He's not just some old man," I said, biting the words through the gasp that was trying to steal my breath. "He's family."

"He's not family," Azrael said. "You keep forgetting that."

Silver moved against linoleum with short double raps. It was easier for me to watch the movement of that crutch he had rather than look into his face. There was something distressing about looking at him full on. It was too familiar and haunting to stare at too long, and it made something in my throat ache. I almost wished he had decided to wear his Birkenstock's and old man grey hair. At least then, he only looked lit up from the inside; this particular facade seemed to pull light toward him and throw it back like a reflective disco ball. If I squinted, I could see prisms dance around the edges of his body. Looking at him full on actually hurt.

"I have to go," I said. "He needs me."

"You're quite wrong," he said. "He *needed* you, and you were there. Now all he needs is a little bit of fluid. A little bit of what humans call medicine, and a little bit of patience. More's the pity."

I clutched at my rib cage, trying to cradle the pain away. "What do you know about what us humans need?"

He made a sound that could have been a tutting noise if he had been an old woman. "You say that as though you still think you're one of them."

I had to grit my teeth through the next wave of pain. It was all I could do to hold onto the chair and suck in air to brace myself.

Azrael seemed unimpressed with my fortitude. Instead he seemed to take great pleasure in the way I was groaning out loud.

"Pity you couldn't keep to your choice of not getting involved," he said, and I imagined I heard harps playing beneath his words. I thought he might be doing that on purpose, and I hated him for it.

"Screw you," I ground out.

"And you seemed so determined before."

I gazed up at him through the bangs of my hair, all the better to filter out some of that incredible light. I didn't want to see him looking dazzling. I wanted to see him looking how I felt. Ragged, hateful.

Another spasm moved through my rib cage. I winced and whatever I had been hoping to say to him, got strangled off in my outcry.

"Too close to the heart," he said, but he certainly didn't sound unkind. To the contrary. He almost sounded sympathetic. "That's what's making this brand hurt."

"Can you make it stop?" I said, taking in short, shallow breaths. I hated the simpering sound in my voice, but I'd take any port in a storm.

He hunched over in front of me and looked up into my face.

"I'm not the one putting it there," he said as though I should know that, but at least he lifted a cool wet cloth to my cheeks. I wasn't sure where he had gotten the thing; I certainly hadn't noticed him going to the sink to run the water over a cloth. At the moment, I didn't care where it came from. Just that it felt soothing against my fevered skin. He swabbed my cheekbones and temples gently, pressing the coolness into the hottest places before letting it linger on my forehead.

"You could've told me," I said, panting through another spasm. "Shit, won't it stop for God sake."

"Told you what?" he said. "That your grandfather had

been diagnosed with an aneurysm?"

My head snapped up at that. Gramp had known? I might have actually been surprised if I hadn't recalled Callum's question to him the night before: whether or not he had told her. Her obviously meant me, and the topic obviously meant the aneurysm. But that Azrael had known? That was disconcerting. I felt more than a little betrayed.

"Well it's comforting to think that everybody knew he was a ticking time bomb except me," I said bitterly. "But I was talking about you telling me some of the more crucial things I needed to know to get through whatever this is that you thrust upon me."

"You say that as though you would have listened to me."

"You could have tried me."

He gave a long, low sigh. He took the face cloth from me and balled it up into his fist. I saw the corner of it dangling from the bottom of his clenched fingers like a tail, and then it was gone. Its disappearance was so quick that it left me wondering if I had seen it or felt it in the first place.

"Do you remember our meeting in the church?" he asked me. "Do you remember what you told me?"

I nodded, miserable. I remembered it well. "I said I had a choice."

His index finger went beneath my chin and he tilted my face to his, but he didn't speak. Instead, a strangely familiar electric shock went through my skin and traveled down my spine, sending little waves out along my shoulder blades. It was as though his touch ignited something deep in my cell memory of the sensation of outstretched wings and in a heartbeat I imagined having them. They were broad and white and soft like gossamer. For another heartbeat, I wished they were still there. Then I realized that he was probably manipulating me the way he manipulated the existence of that face cloth.

Even as I realized it, I noticed the tingle was gone. The burning in my ribs eased up just a bit. I was able to breathe better.

I imagined that sensation was his way of telling me everything he wanted to say and I pulled away from him, gripping the edges of the table so that I could stand on my own two feet.

"I still do have a choice," I said. "But it would've been nice to know what I was up against."

He shrugged. "Had you shown any interest, I would have given you information. I would've told you everything I thought you needed to know."

"Right," I said and couldn't help the sarcasm in my voice. "Because you're so forthcoming."

He leaned his cane between the shoulders of the chair and used it to stand. He crossed his arms over his chest.

"You've always been difficult, Ayla." There was a gleam in his eye as he said it, as though he was both impressed and frustrated at the truth of it. "You might have forgotten your original incarnation, but I haven't. I've known you a long time."

"Spare me," I said. "I really could care less how well you know me. What I really want to know are those things you could've told me when you first branded me."

"Still stubborn," he said. "I told you it's not me branding you."

"Semantics," I said. "What are you keeping from me?"

"So now you want to know," he taunted.

"You have a terribly human nastiness to you," I said. I wanted to hurt him somehow. "For an angel."

As though to prove my point, he glowered at me, but it didn't reach his eyes, and so I doubted he was really angry.

"Your first reap was originally a fallen virtue, like you," he said, and I could swear a smile was playing at the corner, but he didn't give into it. "You do remember what a virtue is responsible for, right?"

I took very deliberate steps over to the refrigerator and yanked open the door. I stood there, letting the cool air from inside bathe my heated skin. Even my collarbone felt like it was on fire.

I could hear him groan behind me and peered over my shoulder. He stood there with both hands on the top of his cane. I had the feeling he was forcing his demeanour to look patient but inside he was seething with impatience.

"What?" I said. "Did you ask me something?"

His lips went into a straight firm line before he lifted his cane from the floor and laid it on his shoulder. "I don't have to give you any information, Ayla," he said. "You're the one asking. So do you want to know or not?"

I sighed. "No. But I suppose I need to know it."

I might have managed to make it all the way over to the fridge, but I couldn't continue standing. I sank down in front of it on my hands and knees, feeling incredibly nauseous for all that. I rolled my head sideways to look at him.

"A virtue is given the power to intercede in the human realm," he said. "Under the right circumstances, and under enough desire and prayer, they can implement things that change outcomes."

My gaze flicked to the doppelgänger. "Are you saying that the power I inherited from that maniac in the church--"

"Fallen one," he said correcting me.

"Are you saying that the power I inherited from that fallen one in the cathedral allowed me to change the outcome of my grandfather's death?"

He lifted his shoulder as though it might be possible, but that he didn't want to commit himself.

"And are you saying," I continued. "That once the outcome was changed, I just sort of naturally reaped the doppelgänger?"

"And have inherited some of his inherent skills as well. Wonderful isn't it?"

"Peachy," I said and managed to find my way onto my bottom and bring my knees up. However I had managed to reap the doppelgänger, I was that much closer to earning back wings I didn't even care about getting back, that much closer to returning to a place I didn't remember, and now I had earned some sort of supernatural aspect I didn't know how to use. The whole entire thing was making my head spin so hard, I was nauseous. I hung my head between them. That felt better. Not perfect, but at least the dizziness was easing. Come to think of it, some of the pain was dissipating too. I could actually take in a long breath without wanting to scream.

"Careful," he said. "Your human body is still susceptible to regular old human things. You don't want to pass out."

"Very helpful," I said.

"I would like to be very helpful to you," he said. "You have so much to learn if you want your wings. Not every creature will be as easy to reap as that one."

I waved my fingers over my head in surrender. "One thing at a time," I said. I couldn't even think about collecting up another entity. The pain of accidentally reaping this one was still riding my nerves.

"Which thing would you like to know first?" His tone was impossibly patient and I looked up at him through my elbows.

"You could have warned me."

There was a flicker of something else behind his gaze, but I didn't understand it. He looked over his shoulder at the desiccated doppelgänger.

"I didn't think you needed me," he said. "Doppelgängers are such stupid things. They have but one task: to warn of death or doom. It's the same thing, really, metaphorically speaking that is."

I felt rather than saw him settle into a chair closest to

the fridge and cross one leg over the other. I peeked up to see him balancing his cane across his lap. I half expected him to wave the tip at the dead thing on the floor and gather it up into some dusty bag. Instead, he watched me quietly as I tried to work out the truth of what was going on.

"My grandfather's doppelgänger," I said. "He didn't even bother to hurt me."

He laughed out loud. "Hurt you?" He said. "I told you they were stupid things. They are opportunistic, parasitic creatures. A doppelgänger wants to live. To do so, even for a short time, it gets its energy from a host that is under threat of death. If the host lives after it bonds, as you saw with your grandfather, the doppelgänger simply passes from existence. But if the host dies, the doppelgänger lives for another season. It finds another host. Why would it want to hurt you? It would gain nothing from it."

I thought about the doppelgänger hovering over Sarah. "So you're sure they can't hurt their host?"

I lifted my head to look at him. His mouth twitched twice. When he swallowed, I could see the muscle movement of his throat and tell it wasn't a conversation direction he wanted to take.

"I suppose one of them can do harm under the right conditions in order to ensure its continued existence."

I looked at him through narrowed eyes. "What if it's been empowered?"

"Empowered," he said with a laugh. "Who would do such a thing? First, it would take a lot of truly nasty spell work and black magic. It can actually be fatal to the person feeding it, since they have to use their own blood to power it."

He pursed his lips together, as though he wanted me to think he had given it all considerable thought and come to a conclusion. "No, a doppelgänger wouldn't be able to harm anyone."

"One attacked me," I blurted out. I might have felt a sense of victory at throwing the information in his face, if it wasn't such a painful thing to recall.

He gave me a strange look. "That's not possible."

"You just said it was possible."

"Under the right conditions."

"But what if the conditions are perfect?"

His sigh was one of resigned impatience.

"Doppelgängers are tied to their host. What host would go to such lengths to empower it with physicality when to do so could only mean death? If it gains corporeality, and the host doesn't look like it's dying fast enough, the doppelgänger will take action to make it so in order to continue existing. So either it kills its host or the strain of giving it corporeality kills its host. Either way, the host dies."

He gave me a suspicious eye and I couldn't meet it. I had a terribly foreboding feeling in the pit of my stomach. The sandwich I had eaten earlier felt like a ball of glue. I didn't think Sarah had been giving me the full story earlier. She let me believe that her family was empowering the doppelgänger when all along it was someone else.

Someone who felt she needed an extra layer of protection.

"What if the person was using their doppelgänger to keep someone from harming her ?"

"A pretty ridiculous and desperate thing to do." He squinted at me. "And that person would have to have a lot of power."

Desperate. That certainly described Sarah.

"What if that person was a necromancer? Would that be enough?"

Those beautifully ice blue eyes nearly disappeared beneath the narrowed slits of his eyelids.

"A necromancer is a despicable thing," he said. "The world is better rid of them."

He lifted his cane from the floor and nudged me in the rib cage where the brand had seared into my skin, and while I had thought he was going to let slide on my seeming desperate interest in a necromancer's safety, he didn't.

"Maybe you don't understand exactly what's at stake," he said. "Both a doppelgänger and a necromancer are supernatural creatures. Your job is to reap them. Not to study them."

My stomach was already feeling queasy again, I was beginning to make connections I didn't appreciate and that terrified me. I prayed the conclusions I was coming to were wrong. I wanted him to tell me differently.

"Just answer the question," I said.

"I am answering the question because there's only one answer. If a doppelgänger is being powered by a necromancer to find physicality, you have to understand where that power is coming from."

The gluey ball in my stomach expanded. "From death?"

He nodded slowly, a patient teacher to a rather slow student. "A necromancer has only one true power. To raise the dead. If your doppelgänger is being powered by a necromancer, and it's gaining corporeality, then what do you think the end result will be? What do you think will be fully physical when the doppelgänger finally decides to end its host's life and extend its own?"

Water flooded my cheeks. I had a horrible image of retching up that big ball of glue and choking on it. My hand went to my stomach instinctively, trying to keep it calm.

He cocked his head at me. "Do you know such a necromancer?"

The way he looked at me, I had the feeling he not only knew the answer, but had known it all along.

I nodded just as slowly and he shrugged as though to say there really was nothing more to discuss.

I didn't need him to explain to me that the doppelgänger had sensed Sarah was in danger and had used it to its own advantage. Whether or not the danger came from a preordained decision she was going to make about using it for protection, she had done exactly that and now she was causing her own demise.

Talk about self-fulfilling prophecies. It was enough to make my head hurt.

"That's exactly what happened," I blurted out.

He tapped his cane on the top of his shoe. "Then if your necromancer is using it to protect herself, not realizing that by giving it power to become physical and harm anyone who would harm her, she's making it worse."

Finally. We were coming to the part I didn't really want to hear. Right back at square one: killing another supernatural creature whether I wanted to or not. I wondered where the next tattoo would appear on my body.

"So I have to stop it," I guessed, and I wasn't surprised to hear the weariness in my tone.

He crossed one hand over the other on top of his cane.

"Stop it?" he said, and he sounded like he thought I had already made the connection and was surprised to hear I hadn't. "No. You have to kill the necromancer."

CHAPTER 16

Kill her. I sagged into a chair. I couldn't do that. How could I? Back in the foster home when I'd had no one, Sarah had been my only family. I eyed Azrael from beneath my bangs. I had a very quick and vivid image of the maniac in the church disintegrating into a cloud of glittery dust that had funneled itself into the top of that cane to remain like that with no sentience, no compassion, no hope. For all eternity.

I had the feeling Azrael had known all along that we were coming to this point and that he knew I would be weighing out the cost of it all. He looked entirely too pleased with himself, and I was willing to bet he assumed I was going to make the choice that suited him. He thought I had no other choice. But there was always a choice. I just had to find the alternative.

He adjusted the cuffs of first one suit sleeve and then the other.

"You're asking for a specific reason, aren't you?" he said, shaking his shoulders into the cut of his suit. "This little necromancer you're so worried about. Sarah."

"She's my friend," I said desperate to explain. Maybe if he understood, he would give me a way out. He'd let this one pass. He'd help me find another option. "I can't just let her die. I can't just let that thing have her."

He leveled me with a blue eyed gaze. "You have no friends, Ayla. You only have targets. The sooner you understand that, the better."

Watching him, I recalled the sad look on the maniac's face when I'd been in the church and he had told me it was over. He didn't want to kill me. He just felt he had to. He had made a choice in that moment to want his wings more than he wanted to stop being a killer. No, I corrected myself. He had made that choice early on and he had reaped what he had sown as surely as he collected the entities he targeted.

I let my gaze trail to the top of Azrael's cane. I wondered what it felt like to be trapped in there for all eternity. I wondered if that maniac felt any pain or if he was just finished.

"I'm not like that maniac in the church," I said to Azrael. "He had already gone too far by the time he came for me. He had no choice. I do." I squared my shoulders, stubbornly peering back at Azrael. "There has to be another way. And if there is, I'll find it."

"You say that as though you believe you still have a choice," he said. "I can assure you, by the end of your days, you'll understand what's at stake. You'll do the same thing as Ozriel."

I shook my head. "You don't know me."

He slipped one hand into his suit pocket. "I do know you, Ayla. You forget how well I know you."

I jabbed myself in the chest with the tip of my finger. "But you don't know this Ayla. You know some angel from eons ago, but you don't know this human I've become."

"You're not –"

"I know," I said, interrupting him. "I'm not human. But that's where you're wrong too. I am human. For all of my time on this earth until I end up in that cane of yours, I will be human. And I will not kill a friend. I will not kill anyone. Not for you."

"That's a pretty speech," he said, smiling. "If you could remember your past at all, I'm sure you'd recall you said the exact same thing when you chose to forget it all and come back again. Something to prove about humanity. Something to prove about the choice you made eons ago."

He waggled his fingers in the air. "You've had lifetimes to prove what you think you understand, and you've never done it. It's time to come home. Either kill the necromancer, or let her die by her own doppelgänger's hand. She will be dying anyway," he said.

"You seem pretty certain of that," I said.

He shrugged. "I'm the Angel of Death," he said. "I know everyone on my list. You kill the necromancer and the doppelgänger dies."

He stood up as though he considered the discussion

over and his business concluded.

"Isn't that what humans call a two-fer?" He pointed at the doppelgänger lying on the floor with the tip of his cane. "This one makes three. Bonus for you."

I crossed the room to stare down at the thing. I had yet to figure out why Azrael hadn't collected it up yet. He was the Angel of Death, after all. Surely, he wanted to store this filthy thing in that cane of his.

"Whatever it is you're going to do with this thing," I said without looking up. "I'm not going to let you do to Sarah."

"She is supernatural," he said. "And she has proven that she's willing to muck about in the natural order of things. That makes her dangerous. You have to reap her."

"She wasn't left with any choice," I said of Sarah. "She was just born that way. Her family is trying to use her and she's trying to resist."

"Weren't you the one trying to tell me there's always a choice?"

I balled my hands into fists and shoved them into my pockets as I glared at him. I hated he was using my own words against me. Watching me, he pushed one hand into his suit pants pocket as he gripped the cane with his other.

"Do you want to see what that doppelgänger becomes as a result of her power?"

I wouldn't answer. How could I? There was nothing I could say that he couldn't counter. Instead, I nudged the thing at my feet with my toe, testing to see how solid it was, if he would suddenly turn into my grandfather's double again.

It did nothing. I could barely move it. I was staring at it, chewing my bottom lip when I felt movement beside me.

I knew Azrael had stepped next to me. His shoulder was touching mine and that electric jolt went through me again. Much like what I felt with Callum, except stronger. I felt a strange longing in the column of my throat. As though I wanted to gulp down gallons of cool water. I was thirsty and starving in the same moment. I had to move away so that he wasn't touching me anymore. Then I turned to look at him, doing my best to keep my eyes pinned to the tip of his cane because his eyes were too penetrating.

I had to back away, get some distance so I could focus. I felt as though I had a fever. Fog was settling around my brain and I had to work through the pea soup to get to the main point. If he was aware of the effect his gaze was having on me, he kept his expression carefully stoic. For some reason that made me even angrier.

"You haven't answered my question," he said, those ice blue eyes drilling into mine.

"No," I spat out. "Of course I don't want that thing alive. I'd have to be just as psychotic as that maniac who had me trapped in the cathedral."

He gave a noncommittal murmur that indicated his own thoughts on the maniac in the cathedral but knew if he voiced them he would put me on the defensive again. He knew as well as I did that I wouldn't want that thing that had attacked Callum and I to be set loose on the world, and he no doubt understood to say so would be to push me too far. Well, it didn't matter. I was already too far on the other side of the fence. And I was tired of it.

"Your list," I demanded. "How long has Sarah been on it?"

He waggled his fingers in the air. "A week or so, give or take. But you know how things go. Nothing is ever certain."

He looked pointedly back over his shoulder at the desiccated doppelgänger who seemed by Azrael's piercing look to destabilize. It put me in mind of fraying papier-mâché. If he was making a point, I didn't understand what it was. I just stood there with my arms crossed over my chest, trying not to think about the consequences of either action.

With a heavy sigh, Azrael twisted away from me and strode over to where the doppelgänger waited. He tapped his cane once on the floor, but he didn't unscrew the top of it this time. Instead, he waited for the doppelgänger to wither into a pile of ash. Then, he blew on it, dispersing the dust into some whirling yellowish portal that he conjured with a swirling motion of his fingers.

"Whatever you decide, Ayla," he said, turning to me with a rueful smile. "Remember that you're not human. Not anymore. You reap witches. You reap necromancers, nephilim, sirens, hell hound, vampires, werewolves, and..."

It was too much. I couldn't take it all in. Somehow, a simple doppelgänger didn't sound so frightening anymore.

The thought that I would have to face things with claws and teeth made me feel as though my veins were shrinking away from my skin.

"Stop," I said.

"You're young now," he said, pressing on with an ever-increasing sense of determination. "But you're still vulnerable. What if you had an accident on that scooter? What if tomorrow you choked on a piece of meat? What will happen to you if you haven't reaped your allotment? Are you prepared for that?" He gave the floor a sharp tap with his cane.

"Dear God," I said, fighting the urge to stop up my ears with the palms of my hands. "Stop trying to scare me."

"Not scare you," he said carefully. "Just explain to you the sense of urgency. Whether you like it or not, whether you choose to seek them out or not, you are a reaper. You never know when an opportunity to reap will be your last. You don't know how much time you have."

I felt as though my throat had gone too tight. I couldn't stop staring at the top of his cane and I believed he was watching me, studying my reaction.

"There has to be another way," I heard myself saying. "I can't do that to her."

He sighed, disappointed sounding. "Always stubborn. Some things never change, even in fresh incarnations." He knocked the top of my boot with his cane. "If you listen to anything today, then at least listen to this: the things that you inherit from the beings you reap will come in handy. I can't help you if you won't be helped, but at least remember that."

With that plea echoing around the room, he was gone and I was left with a strangely empty feeling. I heard a sharp pop coming from somewhere beside me as the portal closed and I collapsed into the chair in the kitchen, peering at the spot where it had been.

It was long moments of sitting there before I realized I was staring at the refrigerator and mulling over his words.

Nothing is certain. Fine for him to say. I supposed an angel with a supernaturally long lifespan, and perhaps immortality, would see one small life as a mere blink of their eyelids.

I knew for Sarah's sake, I would have to face the thing that was draining her, but the thought of doing so made me break out into a sweat. It wouldn't be as easy as Gramp's double because she was powering it. Azrael's last plea wasn't the least bit useful even if he seemed to think it was. What I needed was a weapon, knowledge, or any information about how I could possibly beat it.

I scrambled for my jacket pocket and pulled out my cell phone. I took a few minutes to pack a duffel bag and hoisted it onto my shoulder to carry out to my scooter. I'd exchanged numbers with Callum when we left Sarah at the hospital. I never expected to be calling him at all, and I wasn't sure whether or not he would even answer.

So instead, I left him a message: the doppelgänger is back and he's pissed.

That would be virtually impossible for someone like Callum to ignore, which of course it was. By the time I landed in the hospital parking lot, my scooter steaming from being pushed faster than its limit, he was already standing next to his old beater car.

He looked too tall standing next to it to even be able to fit inside. His jeans were scuffed at the bottom, but he had pulled on a leather jacket that made his shoulders look even broader than they were. For a second, I thought that if he was there, all was forgiven, but then he turned to me and the scowl on his face cut short that little fantasy.

I climbed off my scooter and propped it up. The helmet caught in my hair as I yanked it free of my head and with a sigh, he reached across to untangle a lock of hair from the visor. It was one moment only, but when his fingers touched my cheek, that spot between my shoulders tingled again.

"I saw another one," I said without preamble. Best to pull the band aid right straight off.

His head dropped back and he groaned the heavens. "Seriously? What in the hell is wrong with this town all of a sudden?" Then, as though he had just realized I was standing in front of him, he gripped my shoulders with both hands and peered down at me with intent study.

"Are you all right?" he demanded. His hand went to my jaw and he turned my face this way and that, inspecting. "Did it hurt you?"

I tried to shake my head but barely managed the movement between his fingers. He let go my face and pulled that calm look over his expression again. I realized as I watched that it was very much like pulling down a shade over a window. An act, then. I wondered what was in his past that made him think he had to look so stoic all the time. I crossed my arms over my chest. His impulsive inspection of me bolstered my hope he would want to help with Sarah. So at least my insult hadn't diminished his concern for what was going on.

"I saw it when – when my grandfather –" I gulped down on the words, unable to say how close he had come, and not willing to feel the pain I would have to admit to if I lost him.

To Callum's credit, he didn't wait for me to finish my sentence. Obviously, as a fireman, he had connections I didn't and already knew.

"God, I'm sorry, Ayla," he said. "I mean, I knew he wasn't well, but I didn't expect it to be so soon."

"He's fine," I said, cutting it short because I just didn't want to go there. It was far easier to focus on the notion that I might be able to hurt something than remembering what Gramp looked like lying there on the floor.

"But there was one of those things with him when I got home."

I fiddled with the latches of my helmet as I gathered my courage, and there was a long drawn out silence that felt as electric as the connection between us when he touched me. Even so, it was him who spoke first.

"So?" he said. "I take it that was the one you are texting me about."

"No," I said. "That one is dead."

"Dead?"

I wiggled my head up and down. "And you know what that means?"

"It means we can kill them," he said.

I smiled in answer.

"Then why are we standing here?" He pulled off his jacket, obviously intending to throw it in the back seat of his car. He reminded me of a thug about to throw down. Strangely enough, I kind of fancied that image.

"I have somewhere to go first," I said and Callum nodded.

It was a quick trip to the intensive care unit that I was after, and I fully expected Callum to wait for me downstairs in the lobby, but he followed me quietly to the unit. He gave me a respectful distance, staying at least three paces behind, but I knew he was there and it felt good to think I might have some support should I need it.

I barely dared step up to the reception counter and heard him whispering behind me to go on. I could do it.

I barely got the question out of my mouth when the elderly nurse took one look at me and reached her hand across the counter to touch me on the arm.

"He's already responded to the doctor positively," she said. "Asked for a cup of cocoa if I'm not mistaken."

I couldn't speak for the relief, and as I spun around to deliver the news to Callum I discovered he was already standing there behind me. He spread his arms wide and I stepped into them before I lost the strength in my legs.

His heart thudded against my cheek in a luscious rhythm, and I pressed my ear into it, enjoying the sound. I was awash in that fragrance of soap and musk again, and it felt so glorious, like life and laughter all at once and when he tightened his grip, one palm against the top of my head, pressing me closer, I wanted everything in the world to stop right there. Wanted it to draw out into one long moment that lasted an eternity.

Of course it couldn't.

He eased away from me and looked down with a broad smile creasing his face. "I'm so glad to hear he's doing well," he said.

"Me too," I breathed out.

"Now are you ready to go kick some ass?"

"Hell, yeah."

It was almost as though some magical angel of death had sprinkled luck down over us because Faye was at the nurses' station when we arrived on Sarah's floor. At first, she wouldn't let us in because it was almost time for her meds, and she would be sleeping after that, but Callum, handsome devil that he was, managed to sway her.

We flipped the curtain back and saw things almost exactly as we had left them. Sarah was barely coming around, and the doppelgänger was there. This time, he was squatting in the chair beside her bed, leaning away from her as though something was pushing him. He eyed her with a pretty creepy looking glower, and if she was aware of it, she merely stared up at the ceiling unfazed.

"Sarah," I whispered and flicked the curtain closed behind me. Callum took up station at the foot of her bed. "Are you awake?"

Those blue eyes of hers trailed from the ceiling to the wall and then down onto my face. She gave me a slow, purposeful nod.

"Good," I said. "Good."

"What's good about it?" Callum said. "She's obviously out of it."

"Maybe that's what we need," I said. "At least until we can get her back to her stash."

I stole a glance at the doppelgänger in the chair, hoping it hadn't taken on Sarah's facade again. I didn't think I could stand looking at it again if it was pretending to be her. I shouldn't have worried. When I looked at it, it appeared as its ordinary revolting self.

"Not really an improvement," I muttered and it hissed at me, but at least it didn't move.

"Watch that thing, will you?" I said to him.

I dropped my duffel bag onto the floor and give it a wary eye as I started to undress. I tried not to look at Callum as I turned my back and unbuttoned my shirt.

"I'm going to need you to help me put my clothes on Sarah," I said over my shoulder.

There was a small sound from behind me that could've been both a grunt of appreciation and terror. I smiled to myself, thinking I had put Callum off his usual arrogant stance. I didn't plan to strip down to nothing, just take off my shirt and jeans. I peeled off the pant legs and slipped them over the top of my feet then flung my jeans onto the bed. I turned around to face him wearing nothing but my bra and panties.

I wasn't expecting to see such a look of hunger across his face, and especially not under the circumstances, but he covered it so quickly, averting his gaze to the bed, I doubted I had seen it at all. I started working the Johnny gown down Sarah's shoulders and that was when he finally came to life.

"Nice to see you in the game," I said to him. "Help me with this."

Sarah seemed to understand what was going on and did her best to let us work her hospital gown off of her and replace it with my shirt and jeans. I knew from experience, she wouldn't be embarrassed about either of us seeing her in her underwear. Back in the day, she had pranced around in them plenty, almost daring people to tell her to get dressed.

I, on the other hand, wasn't quite as confident about my own body. But this wasn't the time nor the place to worry about that. I pulled her gown on over top of my underwear and smoothed it down over the front, focusing hard as I looked at her face.

I had no idea what exactly I had to do in order to get my new, mad reaper skills to work and so I did the only thing I could think of. I concentrated hard, focusing on the way her eyebrows looked like dove wings over her eyes. I took in the black fringe of hair and reminded myself she was really a blonde but that she would want to be brunette if she had a choice. Then I smoothed down the gown over the front of my body and looked up at Callum.

"How do I look?"

"Like you're trying to open a jar of pickles," he said.

I think the creature laughed at me.

I groaned. This wasn't working. Maybe I'd misunderstood Azrael. I tried to bring to mind everything he'd said. Nothing is certain. To me that meant Sarah's death wasn't fated. That meant the doppelgänger would be anxious until the time came. It might be antsy. It might make mistakes. It was obviously watching us pretty intently, trying to work out what we were doing. Since it wasn't attacking, it no doubt was recovering what energy it had lost when it had razored through Callum's chest.

But there were been one other thing Azrael had said that stuck in the back of my mind even though I hadn't known what to do with it at the time. He'd said that as part of my new role, I would take on aspects of those supernatural creatures I reaped. That one thing I had counted on was being able to somehow glamour myself into looking like Sarah. My entire plan depended upon it. I could hear the nurse outside the door, talking to Faye, and telling her it was time for Sarah's sedation. There wasn't much time.

Regardless of whether or not I looked like Sarah, it was time for Callum to get her out of there.

I kicked my duffel bag under the bed, telling myself that in the end it would all work out right. It would have to.

"Help me with her," I said again, and lay my hand on Sarah's arm, fully intending to warn her she was about to be picked up and carried out of there bodily. That's when I heard Callum gasp. I looked up to see him staring at me, his mouth open enough that I could see the backs of his teeth.

"Holy hell," he said, skirting a look back over his shoulder at where the doppelgänger was sitting in the chair, its tongue hanging out. "Is that you, Ayla?"

I looked down at my hands, flipping them over for inspection. They certainly looked like my hands, but then hands were hands. I ran my fingers through my hair, pulling it forward into view. Black. Not my regular fiery red, but pitch black like Sarah's dye job. I couldn't help laughing. I felt giddy.

"It worked," I said. "Holy hell, it worked."

I looked askance at the doppelgänger and it seemed as though it had pitched up forward onto the tips of its toes as it rocked back and forth on the plastic chair. It looked like it was about to leap at me, but I knew it wasn't solid enough to do any harm. At least not yet. But it was most definitely getting antsy. I wasn't sure I could trust it to stay where it was.

"Get her out of here," I said to Callum. "Take her back to the crypt. I'll be there as soon as I can."

Luckily, Sarah was aware enough to let him sling his arm over her shoulder and walk her through the curtain. I jumped into the bed and pulled over the sheets just in time to see both the doppelgänger disappear and the nurse flick the curtain aside. I was still settling into place when I heard her say goodbye to Callum and tell him visiting hours the next day would be an hour later.

Success. At least for stage one. I tried to make myself

go limp and looked up at her through veiled eyelashes.

"Time for your sedatives, young lady," she said with a note of cheeriness that made my stomach turn. "Now make sure you swallow them. We don't want any hysterical shouting again tonight."

I tried to offer what I hoped was a drug-induced stare, complete with docile nod. She popped the pill onto my tongue and poured a mouthful of water from a paper cup between my lips. I caught the thing just in time before it washed down my throat and slipped it up between my teeth and my lip. Her finger went to the bottom of my chin and tugged my jaw open. She twisted my face back and forth, inspecting.

"Good," she said. "Sleep well. You get through one night without hollering, and we just might let someone sign you out."

I wished she would stop being so chatty. I was sure that every moment was ticking down like a time bomb and I needed to get out of there. It was an agonizing wait as she fluffed the pillows like a good little nurse and tidied up the bed stand. She snapped the sheets over me and tucked them in nice and tight beneath the mattress. She stood there for several moments with her hands on her hips, surveying the area and then she pulled open the drapes to the rest of the ward and rambled over the other patient in exactly the same way. It was all I could do to keep from groaning out loud and yelling at her to hurry the heck up, but finally she left the room with a flip of the light switch and closed the door.

Finally.

I jumped from the bed and pulled the duffel bag out from beneath it. I waited to see if the other occupant would squeal on me, but she just looked up at me with her finger to her mouth. I stripped off the hospital gown and pulled on the spare set of clothes I had packed. It was only when I was pushing the duffel bag back under the bed that I saw the small leather pouch lying next to my pillow.

The leather pouch. Gramp had sent me that to give to Sarah. We had used it to keep the doppelgänger at bay, and now it was lying here on her bed too far away from her to be of any aid. I thought of the way the thing had disappeared as the nurse had come into the room, and my stomach lurched as I imagined Callum and Sarah finding their way to the crypt.

I grabbed the bag from the mattress and stuffed it into my pocket.

I didn't know if the glamour would still be on me or if I had to do something special to let it release, but I didn't have time to wait. I strode through the ward room and yanked open the door, believing I looked like me and not Sarah. I caught Faye's eye as she sat behind the desk and she nodded to me with a confused look on her face. I took that to mean she thought I had left earlier with Callum and couldn't quite figure out what was going on.

Stage two complete. So far so good.

I got all the way out of the hospital and onto my scooter without incident. The trip to the cathedral was an agonizingly slow one. It didn't matter that I was pushing

Old Yeller to its limits, it couldn't have possibly gone fast enough for me.

I let go a breath of relief when I saw Callum's car parked on the corner of the parking lot at the cathedral. I was already deep in the bowels of the tunnel when I thought to pull the cell phone from my pocket and send out a text. I copied both addresses into the text bar and shot out two words: I'm coming.

A text back seconds later from Sarah's phone: too late.

CHAPTER 17

I raced down the short tunnel toward the crypt with my heart in my throat. I was relieved to see that the sconces in the crevices of the walls in the tunnel were lit and glowing a faint yellow. That was good. I would need to use my cell phone battery to find my way back to the cavern on the other end of the tunnel.

I picked my way along, jumping over stones and running my hand along the side of the walls when I thought I would fall. I knew I was close when my fingers slipped into a crevice along the way and touched on something hard and rough. Yanking my hand away, creeped out by the feel, I shone my cell phone light and had it. It was the same narrow nook housing its complete skeleton that had remained untouched by Sarah's magic the night before. The bones and its skull remained untouched from Sarah's earlier machinations.

At least I was close. Even my stomach seem to sense it.

My bladder spasmed, letting me know it was completely willing to void every bit of liquid at the first sign of danger. I dragged in a shuddering breath and pushed further down the tunnel. They needed me. I couldn't waste any time.

I heard the chattering of what sounded like teeth long before I saw the fallen skeleton army trying to reassemble itself from the floor. The bones were shivering and shaking against each other as they tried to rise and it made the hairs on my arms prickle to attention.

Too late, Sarah had texted. And I saw now that she must be trying to raise her army again. For whatever reason, she was having difficulty. I had hoped that getting her back to the crypt where she had left her stash might give her the tools she needed to control the doppelgänger, but if she was trying to raise the skeletons and they weren't responding, then something had to be terribly wrong.

It took everything I had in me to push open the door. I wasn't sure what I was expecting to see; I just knew that what I wanted to see was Sarah and Callum standing victorious in the middle of the room. I wanted to see the doppelgänger lying dead on the floor. I saw neither of those things.

I was met with the sight of Sarah cringing into a corner. Her hands were stuffed to her mouth, her eyes kept darting to the other side of the room where her cooler lay. She wanted to get to it, that was clear. Something was keeping her from doing it.

I swung my gaze sideways and in a heartbeat saw the reason she couldn't.

The doppelgänger had managed to find enough energy to finally become physical and it seemed intent on staying that way. It had thick daemon-like thighs covered in boils seeping sizzling fluid onto the cavern floor. Its gaping mouth showed all two rows of its razor sharp teeth as it billowed out its fury in her general direction. The long arms ended in thick talons with claws the size of knives.

A wash of dizziness swept over me so fiercely, I only vaguely registered the ringing in my ears.

My bladder threatened to give way.

My first instinct was to back away and run headlong back down the tunnel, but I forced myself to stand my ground. She needed me. She needed me now. I dropped my cell phone and everything in my hands so I would be free to help.

I shouted at the thing, trying to distract it, but it came out as nothing but a squeak. No one noticed me. Not even Sarah. She had eyes only for that thing trying to get to her.

It was only then I realized the only thing keeping it from latching onto her was Callum. With every lunge the thing made, Callum delivered either a kick or a punch and sent it staggering, but he was growing tired. Sweat ran down his brow and his last kick seemed to have a little less energy in it.

The thing roared and I leapt forward without taking the time to think. In seconds, I had thrown myself at its legs, wrapping my arms around its ankle and pulling at it, hoping against hope that Callum would be able to bring it down with his next kick.

That didn't happen. The thing swung its gaze down at me and I swore I saw a recognition in the depths of its eyes. The pain in my bladder was almost enough to beg release, but I managed to hold it as I stared into those yellow eyes.

I knew it was going to swing at me even before the arm came sailing in an arc toward me. When it clubbed me alongside the ear, it was as though it had jarred loose rational thought. What had I been thinking to believe Sarah could simply find the energy to live and disintegrate this thing? She had already empowered it, and it wasn't going to give in to the rules of its existence quite so easily.

I still clung to its ankle, despite the blackness creeping in at the edges of my vision. I couldn't imagine how I was still holding on, even when I felt my shirt ride up and drag against the bare dirt as it lumbered its way toward Sarah.

"Hold on," Callum shouted and I tried to answer with a feeble nod. He needed time, obviously. I desperately hoped he was setting up some massively fantastic roundhouse kick that would knock the thing halfway across the cavern because my grip was slipping and it seemed as though I was nothing but a bit of tissue stuck to its shoe at any rate.

I heard the thud of his foot striking the creature, and I fully expected the doppelgänger to stagger backward. I even let go in anticipation, afraid the thing would fall on me. I managed to find the energy to roll sideways away from it and push myself up onto my elbows and knees. Everything hurt. My breath was nothing but a ragged sound in my ears that battled for precedence over the ringing. I had a hard time holding my head up against the black weight that wanted to take me.

I did look up, and the thing hadn't followed. Callum was standing there, his chest heaving, sweat dripping down his brow. I watched him sway on his feet and the thing laughed at him. Laughed. It thought it had won.

Sarah let go a squeak. She tried to jump out of the way and run toward the cooler. I imagined she thought she could control the thing by now, and whatever was inside that thing might help her. Only I knew she was wrong. Now that it was a corporeal thing, she had lost control. She just didn't realize it.

That was when I remembered the pouch. I had dropped it. Along with my cell phone. How foolish of me. The one weapon that we had, the only thing proven to keep the doppelgänger at bay and I had dropped it like it was a piece of trash. I clambered across the floor, searching frantically with my fingers, praying hands would land on it. My cell phone came first. I pushed it aside. Sarah yelled again. I could hear Callum grunting as he tried to land another kick.

It had to be somewhere. I ran my hands along the floor of the cavern, sideways. Back and forth.

I thought I heard my name being shouted, but I drowned it out. I knew what to do. I just had to find the thing. I heard myself muttering the please dear God let the thing still be working. I prayed there wasn't an expiration date.

I could've wept when my hand ran across the feel of

leather. I fisted my hand over it and rolled over onto my back, yelling for Sarah.

She was pressed as far back into the cavern as she could get, and both Callum and the doppelgänger were already peered closer than they had been. Callum was losing. He was exhausted. Even the doppelgänger seemed to know it and was advancing with a stolid and dogged purpose.

"Catch it," I yelled at her. "And don't move."

I tossed the thing at her. It arced high over both Callum and the doppelgänger, creating a beautiful circle in the air before it landed neatly between her hands. Both he and the creature watched it sail through the air and by the time it was descending, the doppelgänger had realized what it was and had lunged for her. She caught the pouch, and the doppelgänger lurched backward as though someone had hooked it from behind.

"Stay there," I shouted at Sarah.

When I yelled at her, the doppelgänger whipped around. Its gaze landed on me with enough fury to make me gasp. It snarled. Even as I caught sight of its face, it transformed subtly. It was no longer a terrifying looking troll, but something that more closely resembled a man.

A man. I almost let go a nervous laugh until it emitted a horrible howl and flew at me, shifting each second as it ran from a man to that horrible troll. From over its shoulder, I could see Callum realizing what was going to happen and he threw himself at the creature again. As he did, the creature swiped sideways without so much as stalling, and those claws dug into Callum's chest.

I watched, horrified, as he ran the distance with the doppelgänger for several seconds, the claws of the creature still embedded in his chest. I tried to stand, tried to launch myself at them, but my legs went to water and I fell to my knees. Sweet horror of horrors, he was down and the creature was still coming. I had only seconds before it got me.

I managed to squeak out Sarah's name just before its fingers closed around my throat. From the corner of my eye I could see her running for the cooler. But it was too late. There was nothing she could do now.

The thing was inches from my face as the pressure increased around my neck. I thought it might dig those teeth into my cheek, and I found myself wincing, trying to wrench myself away from it, but instead, its face transformed again, showing me the visage of that man's face.

It did open its mouth. It didn't hiss as I expected. It didn't roar like a beast. Instead, it spoke.

"Die," it said.

My bladder finally let go. I felt hot liquid running down my leg and pooling into my shoe.

I went into full panic mode then. I didn't know what Sarah was doing on the other end of the crypt, or what Callum was suffering on its floor. Everything shrank down to that small microcosm of space with the thing's hands around my throat and the pressure that they elicited formed everything I knew.

I was vaguely aware I was kicking and trying to scream. My vision started tunneling down to one pinprick and my chest ached with a burn so incredible, I imagined that was what it must feel like to be on fire.

In the midst of that panic, as the moments stretched themselves out like salt water taffy, Azrael's words flitted through my mind like a butterfly on the breeze. This would be my last incarnation. I would die here. I would end up in the top of his cane because I hadn't reaped all of the things I needed to in order to find my way home.

I knew in that moment that whether or not I wanted to be a reaper, I at least wanted to live. I thought of the very real home I had found in my grandfather's house. The love and comfort he offered me and I kicked in earnest.

A smile slithered across the creature's face. There was evil in his eyes. Deadly intent.

It laughed. It transformed itself fully into that man with a face as beautiful as it was evil looking and laughed right at me.

A man. Glamour or not, the thing holding me was real. It was physical. It had managed to find the corporeality it had been draining Sarah for and was on the cusp of its complete transformation. I thought it strange that all the horrible things he could have become, as Azrael had said, it would choose to become a man. A plain and simple man with all the weaknesses and flaws of a human.

And yet I knew one place men were vulnerable, even if beastly creatures weren't.

Like I had done to the maniac in the cathedral, I lifted

my knee with as much thrust as I could find and it landed directly between his legs. Bastard, I wanted to say. Take that. Suffer. Let me go.

And it did let me go. Just enough that I could kick him again. Mercilessly. Then again. With a vengeance.

He dropped his grip on me and when I kicked him the third time, he fell to my feet. Fully a man for all that. Cradling himself.

I was vaguely aware of a sense of victory, but it wasn't enough. The adrenaline was already soaking my tissues and it was hurtling through my body like a train. I was furious. Righteously angry. How dare it touch me. How dare it come after the people I loved.

I kicked at the thing, shoving it backwards.

I scrabbled for the nearest stone and lifted it high over my head. The creature rolled over just enough it could catch my eye. Something shifted in its depths. Before I could drop the rock down onto the creature, the entire thing shivered and wavered in front of me. It was trying to shift again; I knew it. I imagined it fully intended to slip back into that awful looking creature with double rows of teeth. As a man, it could only do the worst a man could do.

But it was a man. Not a horrible looking creature. A man.

I dropped to my knees next to it with the rock in my hand.

"Do it, Ayla," Callum yelled.

I hesitated. It looked so human. I didn't know how I could go through with it.

"Now," Callum said.

Like the flickering of an old-fashioned TV screen, the creature's body shifted and wavered in front of me. I waited, transfixed, only barely aware of Sarah and Callum yelling at me to finish the job. The thing hissed at me, and although it looked like a human, it sounded like a beast from some nightmare. I lifted the stone high over my head.

Something, some.. One... looked like it was peeling away from the thing's skin. Like a specter from a Shakespearean drama, it started to lift. They were becoming two separate things: specter and doppelgänger, and I realized in that moment that whatever had taken possession of the doppelgänger was trying to escape.

I couldn't let that happen.

I dropped the rock directly onto its skull and I heard a crack as the bones split apart.

CHAPTER 18

The nausea took me immediately.

I crawled away into a corner and retched up everything I had put in my stomach that day. I was vaguely aware of someone holding back my hair and rubbing the back of my shoulders.

It was Sarah's voice that came to me. "It's okay, you're going to be okay."

The last bit of bile collected in the back of my throat and I had to cough to bring it forward. I spit it out onto the floor of the crypt. The sour stink of sick rose to my nostrils and I laid my hand on the wall, hanging over my knees. I was still trying to breathe, to fuel my quaking legs with oxygen. I shuddered without helping it.

I didn't want to look behind me at the thing lying on the floor of the cavern. It looked too human.

"We need to get Callum out of here," Sarah said. Her voice was stronger, much more clear. Her dizziness seemed to be receding and I imagined the adrenaline that no doubt fueled her also swallowed up the residual effects of the medication. I swung my gaze sideways to take in the way she was looking at me with concern across her face. Her eyes darted toward the middle of the crypt, she too, avoiding looking in the direction of the Doppelgänger's body.

"Is he alright," I said, and heard my voice breaking. Every part of my body seemed to tense as I waited for the answer. "The thing didn't kill him did it?"

She shook her head. "He's breathing, but he's bleeding an awful lot."

"We have to call an ambulance," I said, and I felt almost normal uttering the simple words. I thought of the last time an ambulance had come to this place, the way it had carried her out of here. We had come an awful long way just to come right back here.

"I already dialed," she said. "But we don't want them to come down here, do we?"

I sighed. "You're right."

I pushed myself off from the wall and took deliberate, if not shaky, steps toward the middle of the cavern where Callum lay on his side. Dark blood pooled out around his chest. He was clutching it and his eyes were wide as softballs. I knelt down next to him, feigning a calm I didn't feel.

"We have to get you out of here," I said. I looked him in the eyes when I said it, trying to tell him without saying so that we couldn't risk anyone coming down here. They would see that creature looked ever so much like a human man's body and then we would be in for a world of questions we couldn't answer.

"Do you understand?" I asked him.

"I'm not deaf," he said. "Just hurt."

Together, Sarah and I managed to push him up so that he was half sitting and half leaning on us. If he was in pain, he did no more than grunt and as I eyed him cautiously from beneath my bangs, I realized he was biting the bottom of his lip.

We managed to get him to a weak stand, and he slung his arms over our shoulders. We stumbled and staggered our way to the entry and picked our way past the graveyard of fallen bones. We only had to get close enough to the tunnel entrance that no one from the ambulance would come in any further and see enough to decide to investigate further in.

I noticed Sarah plucked one of the bones from the nook where the undisturbed skeleton sat, its skull grinning out at us. Without a word, she shoved it in the back of her pants, beneath the waistband of her jeans and if Callum noticed he was too busy fighting back the pain to say anything.

All three of us collapsed at the entrance to the crypt and that was where the ambulance found us not five minutes later.

I was on my way to the hospital in the back of the ambulance before I realized the Doppelgänger's brand hadn't come. My fingers trailed to my rib cage where the first had burned in. I tried to feel relief that I didn't have to experience a second one, but I couldn't help thinking that I felt cheated somehow.

We had to do a bit of lying about running into a bobcat to explain the deep gashes in Callum's chest, and I wasn't sure if anyone in emergency really believed us. Luckily, when the victim agrees with the story, triage nurses merely look over the patient's head at each other. If they doubted us, they said nothing.

The main thing was that he was going to be fine, and I hadn't realized how much that mattered to me until he was all bandaged up and coming out into the waiting room. There was a spark in his gaze as it landed on me that took the wind from my lungs. I sagged onto one of the hard back plastic chairs.

We were exhausted, all three of us, but I had one more stop to make before I could go home and they seemed to sense it. Callum was the one who headed to the elevator first and punched the button. We trooped into intensive care and they waited outside the door while I went in to see my grandfather.

He was still hooked up to dozens of wires and tubes, but his black eyes landed on me with all the alertness they'd always had. He looked relieved to see me. I clutched his hand a little tighter than I normally would. When he squeezed, I fell across his waist and sobbed until the blankets beneath my cheeks grew wet.

It wasn't until I felt someone standing behind me that I sucked in the tears and peered over my shoulder.

"The nurse says he's doing remarkably well," Callum said.

I nodded. I felt as though I could finally breathe.

Gramp seemed to look a little less pale than when I'd first come in. I ran my hand through his hair, smoothing it down around his ears were the tubes made it stick up.

"I can leave you alone with him," Callum said, "if you want to talk to him in private."

I shook my head.

"I can't do it alone," I said. It was a hard admission, but I felt stronger with Callum there. There were plenty of things I wanted to say to Gramp. I wanted to tell him I didn't know what I would do if I had to live without him, that I would rather spend an eternity in the top of some angel's cane before I let anything happened to him. That he was the most important thing in my life.

I swallowed down all those words because they didn't seem to contain exactly what I felt.

"You're a tough old fart," I said to him.

The ghost of a smile played at the corners of his mouth.

Callum went around to the other side of the bed and I watched Gramp's eyes follow him.

"They're going to take all those tubes out of him tomorrow morning if he keeps this up."

"The nurses better watch out then," I said, feeling as though someone had taken a very heavy cloak off my shoulders. "Don't argue with them when they bring you oatmeal," I said. He hated oatmeal. He lifted his hand from the sheets and made a motion like he wanted to drink.

"Water?" I asked.

He shook his head and made the motion again.

"Cocoa," Callum said and Gramp touched the tip of his nose with his index finger. I couldn't help but smile.

"Maybe when you're all divested of those restraints," I said with a chuckle. It felt good. Liberating. For the first time in days I imagined things could actually look up.

I gave Gramp's hand a short squeeze then pushed myself to my feet and shoved my hands in my pockets. I felt as though I could sit there and watch him for hours, just seeing that chest rise up and down as he inhaled and exhaled. I hadn't thought about his mortality until the moment I realized he was mortal. I hadn't thought about mortality at all. Ever. When my parents had died in that car crash, I had just sort of shut down. Death wasn't something that happened to your own parents. It was some unfortunate event that happened to someone else. While I'd been unequipped as a young teenager to deal with it then, I had the feeling with his near miss that whatever I hadn't processed all those years ago was going to come back fourfold. I wanted my grandfather around to help me through it.

One thing nagged at me, though. One thing still unexplained that he would have to divulge when all this was over and he was feeling better. I couldn't ask him then, but I wanted him to know he still had some explaining to do.

"Rest assured," I said to him, smoothing over his

sheets. "You're gonna tell me what was in that bag."

"That's easy," Sarah said from behind me. I turned around to see her leaning into the room, peering around the door frame.

"The same sort of stuff that's in every malice bag," she said. "Although I'm not so sure you want to know how he has such a thing."

"I don't even know what that is," I said and looked sideways at Callum. He shook his head, as oblivious as I was.

Her chin seesawed back and forth and I had the feeling she was trying to decide how much to tell me. I sighed.

"Go ahead," I said. "You might as well tell me."

"It's made with witch's hair."

I noticed her gaze flicked to Gramp where he lay on the bed. In response, my grandfather squeezed his eyes shut as though he had suddenly been taken by a Rip van Winkle need for sleep.

Compared to all the other things I had experienced in the last few days, that actually didn't sound too bad.

"Simple enough," I said and Callum echoed my sentiment, although I noticed he too flicked his gaze to my grandfather's face.

"Well there's something else inside too," she whispered, her voice going harsh in the quietness of the room.

"How bad is it?" Callum said over my head. There was an almost macabre sort of fascination in his eyes as he asked. I would have thought he'd had enough of supernatural things as well. The drawn outlook in his face certainly said so.

Sarah leaned in toward him, rasping out the words and I noticed Gramp flinching as she spoke.

"A little bit of liver or little bit of heart. It's never the same. But it's always from the same witch who donates the hair."

"You say donate, but.." I trailed the last of the sentence off because I had a hard time contemplating how he'd come into possession of it, let alone saying it out loud. A person couldn't exactly donate their liver or their heart.

"Bingo," she said. "The witch would need to be dead," she said. "Which means that your dear old Gramp here knows a little bit about sorcery and magic, and not the lovely white unicorn kind either."

I caught Callum's eye and saw in their depths a look of disbelief that must have mirrored my own.

I dropped my gaze to Gramp. I saw him peeking out through one squinted eye.

"Druid, huh?" I said. "It sounds to me like that's just a cover. Maybe someone has a secret."

Gramp's mouth twitched around the tubes.

Sarah came up beside me. She ran her hand over Gramp's heart, her fingers fluttering in midair as they hovered over his solar plexus. "Actually," she said. "Druid magic is quite complex and can be quite dark at times. I'm sure he's telling you the truth."

She looked at me sideways. "And since that seems to be the case, I'd bet that would make your house a perfectly safe place for a necromancer who has nowhere else to go."

I couldn't imagine what Azrael would say when he realized I was housing a druid as well as a necromancer. I kind of wanted to tell him just to see the look on his face.

I looked to see her grinning at me and I realized exactly how afraid she had been in the crypt. She looked like her old self again, back before the government services tried to send her home. She reached out for my hand and I felt her squeeze it.

She looked at me with a plea in her expression even though she should have known perfectly well that I didn't need for her to ask. It wasn't up to me, though; it was up to Gramp.

The nurse poked her head in the door. She looked annoyed as she took in the amount of people hovering around Gramp's bed.

"I'll leave," Callum said.

"You all need to leave," the nurse said.

I didn't want to go, but had to.

"You need to sleep," I said to him. "I'll be back later."

His hand snaked out and gripped my elbow. He tugged on my arm. When I turned to look at him, I realized he was doing his best to pucker up around the tubes.

With a small clucking sound, I pecked his forehead with a kiss. He caught my eye as I pulled away and flicked his gaze toward Sarah. I got the message immediately.

"You can have my room," I said to her. "I'll stay in Gramp's for now."

The relief that crossed her face was palpable. And I

realized how good it felt to have a friend again.

I left the hospital with the sense that something still hung over my head, but I decided to shelve that particularly unsavory feeling until I had more energy.

All I knew was that I needed to get home. I needed to see the familiar 70s wallpaper and the line of pictures going up the stairs. I needed to drop on my bed and fall asleep for a million years.

CHAPTER 19

I woke several hours later with a telltale pain in my ankle. The only light in the room was the yellow glow from Gramp's old-fashioned digital alarm clock. I shot up in bed, gripping my foot with both hands and doing my best to bite down on the moan working its way through my throat. I rocked back and forth on the bed, cradling my ankle in the vain hopes the pain would recede. It occurred to me, as a fresher wave crested up my calf, that this was exactly what I had felt hanging over me. I should have known I couldn't escape it for long.

Azrael came when the pain was at its worst. and he rode it out with me. He held my hand through it all and squeezed my fingers to distract me. Every now and then he caught my eye and while I thought that wry twist to his mouth would be to mock me, he said nothing until the pain was done. Then he pushed himself to his feet, brushing his suit free of wrinkles and stood looking down at me.

He looked too compassionate for my taste. I wanted to hate him. I had to remind myself he was the reason I was suffering.

"What took you so long?" I bit out.

"You needed your sleep," he said and ran his fingers through the black forest of hair so that it waved delicately around his ear lobes. That peculiar light edged his body again, and I could swear I heard harp music.

"I prefer you looking like an old man," I said. Being woke up in the middle of the night was bad enough, but being rattled awake by pain in the presence of the Angel of

Death was most decidedly not on my fantasy list.

His chuckle was like the sound of a harp being plucked in all the wrong places. I glared up at him from the bed. The pillows behind me bundled up against my back in an uncomfortable way.

"If you knew I needed my sleep, why didn't you just wait until morning?" I flipped the blankets back and limped over to the light switch. I took perverse pleasure in snapping it on, hoping he might have to blink away at the sudden light. He didn't. The only one left squinting in the glare was me.

He chuckled and tapped my bed with the tip of his cane. "Spiteful even in your human flesh," he said. "Come have a seat."

I crossed my arms over my chest. "I prefer to stand."

He pulled his suit legs up at the knee and eased himself down on the edge of the bed and let me look down on him. I got the feeling he was trying some warped reverse psychology. The cane propped between both knees with both his hands on the top. I noticed how elegant those fingers were as they curled around the grieving angel.

"It's done then," he said.

I nodded, not trusting my voice.

"But no necromancer," he said.

"You really thought I would reap her?" I said.

He lifted an eyebrow. "Actually," he said. "I would've been surprised if you did."

"Damn straight," I said and glowered at him. "What in the hell was that thing?"

"Which thing, exactly?" he said in a frustratingly naive voice. Then he laid his cane against his chest and lifted his hands to count the fingers on one hand. "There's the druid in the hospital bed," he said. "Then there's the necromancer, the doppelgänger the –"

"You know exactly what I'm talking about."

"Do I?" He pushed himself to his feet with his cane and moved near enough to me that I could smell the candy floss on him. The sky blue of his eyes shifted to an almost purple iridescence and I could make out the shifting images of clouds and sky and Earth and wings in them as he looked at me.

For a moment, my mind fed me an image of him in a beautifully gilded room. He was reaching out to me with a sad smile. I had the feeling that I wanted to lay my cheek against his chest, and feel his palm against my hair. Then as quickly as the image came, it evaporated. I was left staring into those simple, but beautiful, blue eyes again.

If he had any idea what had just run through my mind, he gave no indication. He just tapped his cane once on the floor to get my attention.

"Do you have any idea how many supernatural things," he said, "actually, how much power, is in this little town of yours?"

I shook my head.

"An entire choir of angels fell here eons ago. That in and of itself gives the ground a powerful energy, but it's the other things attracted to that energy that make this town what it is. It's why your little necromancer chose this town to hide in."

He turned away from me to stroll across the room. He ran his fingers over the items on my grandfather's bureau when he stopped in front of it. Several pictures, propped in their frames, sat clustered together. I recognized my mother in one of the frames. She looked beautiful. Red hair like mine, the bright blue eyes of a pre-teen. Freckles dotted the top of her nose and in the spot between her eyebrows. I felt the familiar clenching of my stomach when I looked at her. As usual, the feeling made me uncomfortable enough that the sting behind my eyelids forced me to blink. I yanked my gaze away from it.

I faced him with defiance.

"So you're telling me this is the perfect place for me to collect all of those things you keep in the top of your cane."

He looked at me, disappointed. "I told you only the fallen ones return to me. I'm sure you remember that. You're stubborn, but you're not stupid."

I crossed my arms over my chest. "Whatever," I said. "You've done your little chore. I've got my brand. You can go now."

He had the grace to look hurt.

"I wish it was as simple as that, Ayla."

"I'm not going to hurt Sarah," I said. "For pity's sake, I only managed to kill that thing in the crypt by some lucky strike. The least you could've done was given me some sort of mad skills to make it easier."

"If it was easy and without risk, then every fallen one would scramble to do what you're doing."

I crossed my arms over my chest and snorted. "This wasn't exactly something I scrambled to sign up for."

"Maybe not consciously as a human," he said. "But there was that part of you that remembers your origin and wanted to return to it. Can you honestly say that when you were with your reaper in the cathedral that things didn't feel familiar? That you didn't sense something that felt right?"

I thought back to those moments, felt again the recollection of familiar words, the sense of déjà vu.

"Even so," I said, stubborn. "You've given me no information. Cryptic remarks that barely help me. If you want me to do this thing, why can't you give me the information I need to know? Why can't you tell me what weapons to use? Why do I have to figure it out on my own?"

There was a moment when it looked as though he was chewing his lip, uncertain. But when he spoke, it was with all the confidence of before.

"It was the angelic host that petitioned the Divine One for this penance," he said. "We felt betrayed. The Divine One wanted to gather you back, but we asked for your punishment. You were from our host. We wanted to be sure that when you returned, you returned only because you truly wanted to. Each of us, even the fallen ones agreed that the task was difficult enough, it would only encourage the truly repentant."

"I don't remember any of that," I said feeling as though none of this was fair. I hadn't exactly been happy as a mortal, but at least I was ignorant. Ignorance had its own stubborn bliss. "And I certainly didn't ask for this."

He stepped closer, wafting that sugar smell over me again. "Which makes it even more urgent, Ayla," he said. "It puts you at more risk. You will be tested. Your mettle will be tried most heartily."

"I've never been good at tests," I said. I meant it to come across a shade defiant, but as I said it, it almost sounded like defeat.

He chose to ignore that and instead lifted the picture of my mother from the bureau. He gave it slow, careful inspection, tracing her face with the tip of his finger before he put it back down on the bureau, face down.

"While you think you have been given a bad lot, I assure you, you'll thank me at the end of it."

Suspicion whispered its way up my spine. I took an unsteady step toward Azrael, testing the strength of my legs, hoping to find they were strong enough to kick him in the shins. I managed to get close enough to him to smell that cotton candy scent again, the one that made me think of pink cumulus clouds and down feathers.

"You knew this would all happen, didn't you?" I said. "You planned it."

"To be truthful," he said. "I hadn't expected things to turn out quite as well as they did."

The way he said it, as though it had been a plan he had carefully concocted and carried out with finite perfection, I realized the breadth of his involvement and what it meant to my traumatic time in the cathedral. What it meant to what was happening now.

"Oh my God," I said, realizing the breadth of what he was saying. "You set me up. It was you."

My fingers jabbed into his chest. "I've been trying to work out why that thing was in the cathedral at the same time I was. How did it know I was there? How did it know what I was?"

I drilled him with my gaze. "It was you all along, wasn't it?"

I might have thought plenty of nasty things about him in this penance that had been thrust upon me, but I hadn't expected a betrayal this deep. It had been happpenstance. I had accepted my lot because I thought it was coincidence, that I had been thrust into it as a result of an accidental meeting. Now that I realized it had been carefully plotted out, I was furious.

"You led it to me," I choked out, realizing the breadth of what had really happened and felt such desolation that I could barely manage the rest of the words. "You sent it to kill me."

He almost looked as though he was sagging in front of me. Everything in his posture pulled inward and his voice went strangely soft.

"Never," he said and there was a strange longing in his voice that confused me. "I would never have done that to you."

"Are you saying it wasn't you who told that thing where I was?"

"I did," he confessed. "But not because I wanted it to

kill you. Mind you, it might have been easier if I had bothered to consider your innate obstinance. If I had, I might have encouraged him to kill you. At least then you could have returned after your human death to the pool of incarnation and I might have coerced you into returning with your full memory. I wouldn't have had to trick you then."

His face looked so earnest; the note of regret in his tone so authentic, I couldn't help but believe him. And I struggled with all the possibilities, trying to work my way through the fog that settled over me as I looked at him. There was only one conclusion I could come to. The truth of it hit me like a sledgehammer in the chest.

"You wanted me to become a reaper."

"Yes," he nearly hissed. The admission was more vehement than nasty. He stepped closer to me, too close. There was nothing but a breath between us, one that sizzled with tension. If I had thought he was magnificent looking before, in the moment he touched me, everything in the room lit up. He was like cotton candy and crystallized maple syrup and light winking through the crests of a wave on a sunny day. I went dizzy with longing, but I had no idea what that longing was for.

"Come home," he said. "Do these things and come home to me, finally."

For a second, I felt as though something soft and fluffy had encircled me, pulled me close and brushed against my cheek.

"It's time, Ayla," he said. "You've been away for too

long. This is your chance to come back to the host. Be yourself again."

Home. To him. To a place I didn't remember and that meant nothing to me. When all I knew was here and where everything that mattered to me wore human skin and was fueled by mortal hearts. I shook my head, trying to work out why I would even want to succumb to the life of a reaper. The fear of his cane wasn't enough to replace the sense of loss that would consume me if I ended up putting the people I loved in harm's way, as I had just done. Callum, Sarah, my grandfather: all of them had a brush with death. Because of me.

I shook my head, trying to work through everything he was saying. He mistook the confusion for refusal.

"You're telling me you would rather stay here," he said and there was a bitter note to his voice that I didn't think an angel could possibly feel. It confused me enough, made me feel sorry for him enough, that I reached out and without thinking lay my palm against his cheek. It seemed to encourage him enough to put his hand over top of mine.

"You'd rather stay here with that abomination when you should be reaping him and sending him to oblivion. Him and that necromancer."

"Tully," I said. "His name is Tully." I hadn't used my grandfather's name in so many years, it sounded strange. So strange, even Azrael cocked his head at me, bewildered.

I pulled my hand from his and he tugged at his cuffs, squaring his shoulders. Businesslike again.

"Whatever you choose to call him," he said. "You're too

far in now, Ayla. There's no hiding anymore. That creature your friend roused..."

"Roused?" I echoed, catching onto that one word because it sounded decidedly dire. "I killed the thing. I have this damned brand to prove it."

"You killed the doppelgänger," he said carefully. "But the thing your necromancer roused with her magics, is far worse than what you executed."

"Whatever we roused," I said, defensive and argumentative. "Is someone else's problem." I jabbed him in the chest again. "It's *your* problem."

"Not mine," he said. "You're the one wearing the tattoos. It will come for you because it believes you are a threat. "

"I only have these tattoos because the people I loved were in danger."

"Well you can trust that it will use those you love if it needs to. Imagine what could happen to that abomination who loves you."

"Is that a threat?" I said, the anger rising. "Because my grandfather is not an abomination."

"Not your grandfather," he said and cocked his head at me. "You don't know, do you? The boy. The one who is falling in love you."

Falling in love with me. Callum. Had to be. There was no one else in my life that it could be. I almost didn't dare hope, but I knew it had to be true. I pulled my arms around my midriff and squeezed. The euphoria was almost too much to contain. Loved. Callum loved me.

I wanted to sag onto the bed and revel in the knowledge, but the beastly angel kept talking. The trouble was, if any of the words had meaning, I didn't register them. I could only think of those four words. I repeated them in my mind until I felt the cane tap against my calf and looked up to see Azrael staring at me.

"Love makes us vulnerable," he said. "And those things with evil intent have no problem using that vulnerability to their own ends." He eyed me speculatively, as though waiting for me to agree when he knew full well I wouldn't. In the end, he gave up waiting and sighed.

"Mind you," he said, moving his finger through the air to connect dots I wasn't seeing. "It would be far more profitable for you to reap the three of them yourself than let them live with the risk of always being bait. At least that way you would be closer to coming home."

He tapped onto an invisible speck in front of my face and waited. He made a popping sound with his puckered mouth.

I thought of Sarah down the hall and of my grandfather in his hospital bed, Callum driving home in his beat up GTI, all the three people I cared about and wondered how much danger they were truly in. If not from me, from that creature we had roused. And if not from that creature, then from some other fallen angel seeking a way home. Then it hit me. I'd connected the dots he seemed to be so adamant that I draw lines to, but I had the feeling I hadn't come up with the same picture he had hoped for.

If the town of Dyre was so full of energy and of

supernatural beings, how long would it be before others like me made their way here, looking for a crowded room to tap out a few stamps on their coupon card?

"Are you one of those things using them for your own ends?" I said, meeting his gaze and holding it. I put all the fire I felt in my chest, all the passion and fear of the last 72 hours in my voice as I spoke to him because I wanted him to understand completely my intentions. I didn't want there to be any doubt in his mind about where I stood.

I gripped him by the lapels.

"Because if you are, you need to know that if anything comes for them, whether it's you or something revoltingly evil or even another Nathelium out to win its wings, I will fight heaven and hell to protect them."

I let him go and he eased away with a smug look he only barely concealed with a short and timid smile. He tapped his cane on the floor and then used the tip of it to press into my solar plexus. Dozens of images swirled around behind my eyelids, but although none of them joined together to create one cohesive picture, I came away with one certain thought. Something *was* coming. And it would do anything to find its revenge.

"How long?" I said and when he didn't answer, I reached out again but instead of gripping his lapels, I lifted the hair of the back of his neck and coiled it around my fist. I wasn't going to let him go. He couldn't get out of there without telling me what I needed to know, and if he tried to leave, he was taking me with him.

"How long before something comes for Gramp or

Sarah?" I asked him.

He gave a short shake of his head and my fingers passed through his hair as though they were nothing but feathers from a down pillow caught in his locks. He brushed my hands away ever so gently and crossed them at the wrists over my hips. His touch lingered a little too long on my skin and I felt the electricity of it winging its way up the nerve endings to the back of my shoulder blades.

"You're forgetting someone," he said. "The Nephilim."

"I don't even know what that is," I said. "Let alone who it is."

"Born of Angels," he said. "A half breed. An abomination that never should have existed. Pretty alluring bait to an entity in need of power."

I shook my head at him, confused. "I don't know what you're talking about."

"The boy," he hissed. "That awful abomination with the power of angels in his blood. Don't think your necromancer won't tap it to save herself. Don't think the beast you've roused won't use it for revenge. Don't think the druid won't use it to fuel a spell in a vain attempt to rescue you if he knows what you are."

I sagged onto my grandfather's bed and stared at the picture of my mother lying face down on his bureau. For the first time since the accident, I found myself longing for her embrace. I felt tears burning behind my eyelids as I thought about where she might be, what kind of eternity she was living through. I'd always told myself that someday I would see her again. Now I knew if I didn't do as Azrael bid, I never would.

I was spent. Exhausted. Afraid, even, but he wouldn't stop. Dear sweet heaven, he wouldn't stop.

"Reap them, Ayla," he said. "You can't let them put your eternity at risk."

Callum was Nephilim. An abomination. One more creature that Azrael would want me to reap in order to earn my wings. Three of them now. Gramp. Sarah. Callum. All people I cared about. People I would die for. People who cared about me. And in front of me, an eternity inside a grieving angel cane handle as a bit of glittering dust never to feel or love ever again.

I thought of Sarah down the hall and of my grandfather in his hospital bed, Callum driving home in his beat up GTI, and I realized that the small family I had left was worth every risk.

And if something came for them, including Azrael or any other Nathelium out to win its wings, I would tear whatever passed for a supernatural soul from their bodies with my teeth.

Azrael seemed to sense the shift even as I looked up at him. A small, sad smile moved across his mouth.

"I'm sorry, Ayla," he said. "I truly am."

Then he was gone and I was left to stare at the empty space where he had stood until the burning behind my eyelids turned to a flood of tears and I clenched at the bedspread with fisted hands.

I didn't move for long moments, not even when my cell

phone blinked on from across the room. A text, no doubt. Probably from Sarah. Maybe from Callum.

And it was only by looking at the way it winked at me from across the room that I found the strength to push myself to my feet and shuffle across the room to pick it up. That one small action reminded me that it was little things like answering a text in the middle of the night, done for the right reasons, that could change a life.

At that moment, I knew my life would never be the same.

<<<>>>

THANKS FOR READING

Authors You Should Try:

I'm sharing the love here, and I'm hoping you will too. I'm listing a few amazing authors I really love because they are kind and compassionate and just plain generous with their time and support. Please check a few of them out if you will. Maybe search for them on social media. Better yet, sample their work: I KNOW you will love it.

Debra Martin, author of *Silver Cross* can be found at: http://twoendsofthepen.blogspot.ca/

Jason McIntyre author of the *Night Walk Men* can be found at: http://www.thefarthestreaches.com

Richard Taubold, author of *The Mosaic* can be found at: http://ricktaubold.com